Impending Earth

By

J.R. Clark

Copyright © 2016 Jonathan Clark
All rights reserved, this work is fiction, all names, characters, locales, and incidents, are products of the author's imagination and any resemblance of actual people place or events is coincidental or fictionalized.

Published in the United States by Clarkltd.
PO Box 45313 Rio Rancho, NM 87174
info@clarkltd.com

Edition 1
United States Copyright Office
#1-3438323231
Library of Congress Control Number: 2017907317
International Standards Book Numbers
ISBN-10: 0692720626
ISBN-13: 978-0692720622
ASIN: B01FVBFXNG
181227

Acknowledgments

To my Father Robert without your never-failing sympathy and encouragement this book would have never been finished;

Furthermore, to all my future readers,

Thank You.

PROLOGUE

I remember the way the sky looked back home: its purple and orange hues in the depths of night, and its vibrant yellows and blues at the height of day. Sometimes, when the sun and many moons threatened to make acquaintance for that brief period before nightfall, streaks of peaceful greens would breathtakingly illuminate the entire expanse.

But that was back home. The greens do not come here, though the skies are wonderful in their own unique way. It is still not quite the same.

Three moons lit our night skies back home. We named them Initius, Magnus, and Fortitus, for the first to rise, the strongest to shine, and the last to disappear in the morning hours. I miss our moons still, and I long dreadfully for the way things used to be, but I do not miss what my home had become in the last days, the days before we were forced to leave in an effort to save our very lives.

My entire existence at home was, at one time, filled with peace; the lives of myself and my three friends, even though we were considered four of the 'middle dregs' of our society, were peaceful.

I have much to share about our former home, and more to tell regarding why we are no longer there. Oh, how the pride that inhabits the living can direct their souls and choices if they allow it! It is this very pride, this lack of both internal and external consciousness, that demanded we flee for our very lives, and this is the story I will relate to you now.

My name is Dyzek, and I and my three companions come from the planet Marmara in the Copetus galaxy. At one time, many, many moons ago, all of the peoples of Marmara were free, but it was that very freedom, the ability to choose and speak so freely and as we wished, which resulted in our need to conduct our own great escape.

I record these truths for those of the future, my 'children', so to speak. The four of us, my 'family', desire for those who will come after us and inhabit this new-found world to learn of this murderous pride which occupies the heart and soul of every being in our species.

We hope they will learn it and keep it tucked tightly away in the depths of their persons, controlling it and keeping it out of their lives.

There may not be another world to run to if our history repeats itself…

Impending Earth

CHAPTER 1

My new family, my friends, and I were all born in the village of Shalbria in the Marmaran country of Diabastus. Camira is my female counterpart and my partner in this life. Barsam is my best friend and right-hand man, and his female counterpart and companion is Morgayne. Since our society changed to suit the needs and desires of the 'perfect' in mind and appearance, we have been considered outcasts, along with countless other Marmarans who did not live up to the standards of those who tailored the rules.

Camira is my pride and joy. She is smart, funny, and outspoken, with long black hair that hangs straight and reaches the small of her back. Her skin is the color of the rich tan sands that run along the coasts of Diabastus, brown and creamy. She has high cheekbones and black eyes that slant slightly at the corners. I adore her entirely.

Sometimes I have to help her to remember to hold her tongue, and this fact makes me smile inside, for I love this most about her.

Barsam has very dark skin, almost the color of mud. His eyes and hair are also black, but his hair has a much coarser texture than that of my love, Camira. He, too, is knowledgeable, and it is with my friend and brother Barsam that I am able to plan and confer in regard to the four of us and our futures. He gives me the best, most honest feedback and advice when it comes to making decisions regarding our day-to-day lives, and I trust and depend on him without limits.

Morgayne is Barsam's, true love. Her skin is lighter than Camira's, but not as light as my own. She has deep brown eyes that slant beautifully at the corners, a bit like Camira's, and her hair is long and black, like that of my own lover's as well. Morgayne is quiet and introspective, and she looks to Camira often for guidance and sistership. They are the best of friends, and Camira considers it her task to protect her more silent sister.

My skin is the whitest of us all, and my hair is yellow. It hangs just below my shoulders in waves, and Camira loves to run her fingers through it. I let her often, and I revel in the chills that the tips of her fingers generate when she caresses it. My eyes are the color of the daytime sky. To put it simply, I do not look like I fit in with the rest of my clan, but then again, none of us look exactly alike, and we should not. Each of us are different in appearance but beautiful unto ourselves.

∞

In the beginning, we were merely close friends. The village of Shalbria was small, and the four of us lived only steps from each other with our families. As children, we sought each other out every minute of the day, and together we would indulge in the whims of innocent childhood. We played games by the nearby river and swam with happiness in its depths. The four of us pretended to be grownups in our games, and we adored each other without harshness or judgment.

All those years ago the individuals who governed our world ruled with the belief that all of us were equal. There was no determination of superiority taking place; no judgment calls that stated one was any better than the other. I remember that all the people of Marmara were very happy, and we lived in harmony. That is not to say that there were no issues. Some people were simply bad from the inside out. Laws were required to maintain safety and order, but those of us who were honest and hardworking abided by the law, and therefore, the law and the punishments it carried were respected and appreciated. But there came a time when all of that changed, and all of us initially thought the change would be for the better.

Oh, but on the contrary! It progressively made things much worse.

You see, Marmara, the planet in its entirety, was handled by the people, with a leading representative who was chosen because our people believed that the chosen individual would hold our best interests at heart. Each leader was decided only after close scrutiny, and the adults of our world took the responsibility of determining each new representative very, very seriously. For the majority of my life, this person was chosen only on how he would lead the people as one, not by what he could offer a select few.

When I started to become a man, those with more tradeable currency and possessions began to control who was chosen to lead.

It all started when our world, Marmara, was visited by the inhabitants of Washa, the closest world to our own. They visited by means of a machine they created which allowed them to travel from planet to planet by what they referred to as 'teleportation'.

The Washans came to share with us the discoveries they had made regarding governing their own people, as well as population control. At the time, this was much-welcomed information. While our country, Diabastus, did not really have any particular issues in these areas, there were other locations in Marmara which did, and they had significant problems as a result. The Washans claimed that they had been observing us from afar, and they were very familiar with our struggles. They offered us answers which consisted of their own unique solutions.

So our people began to welcome the differences with open arms, even we peaceful Diabastians. Being on the high end of the pole of existence became paramount to everyone, as the Washans had begun to breed fear in our hearts, fear of each other and what could potentially take place between us. This fear became the strong point in all dealings, even in places where it really should not have mattered at all. Value was then placed on high intelligence and physical beauty and strength. If people were sick or unappealing to the eye, they were shunned. If they could not keep up with common mental challenges, they were included with the 'unwanted'. Worst of all, if you were associated in any way with those found lacking, you were grouped together with them and judged by the same standards, regardless of your own personal abilities or looks.

Though subtle, the use of this plumb-line was the beginning of the end for our world, and we Marmarans were none the wiser, unfortunately.

Those who believed firmly in the old ways, the ancient traditions for choosing representation, such as my parents and the parents of my current clan, disliked the Washans. They did not trust the motives of our visitors, nor did they believe in the way the Washans determined personal value in individuals. I remember overhearing my own parents discussing the 'New Way' for the very first time.

∞

I was standing in the corridor of our home, and their voices were echoing from the room where we took our family meals together. It was not their words which captured my attention, but rather the urgency of the tones of their voices. They were angry and concerned.

"Matsia," my father began, speaking to my mother. "I have a sense of dread for the future. The teachings of the Washans are bad for the spirits of all Marmarans. Evil is spreading in some, and it even touches their eyes."

There was a pause before my mother spoke. "Yes, my dear. I am afraid I agree with you. Already the people are leaving the village of Shalbria and taking off to the foothills of Eloques for safety. I fear we may need to join them."

I had walked out into the open then, into their presence. As soon as my parents took notice of me, they both smiled and pretended that they had not a care, but I had heard their voices, and from that day on I began to pay very close attention to the doings of those in charge of Marmara and all of its countries and villages. I began a personal vigil: if my parents were concerned, I should be too, for I trusted them implicitly.

In the beginning, they never spoke to me personally about the topic, but I watched their faces and listened to their conversations from afar. I knew that if the time ever came to 'run for the foothills' they would let me know, but I wanted to be ahead of the game.

∞

After hearing that first brief exchange between them, I had gone to my three friends. We had sat along the banks of the river near the outskirts of Shalbria staring at the light of the sun as its rays bounced off the surface of the water playfully. The sun had not a care, for it was not being judged. It was taken for granted.

"I overheard my parents speaking amongst themselves regarding the state of our government and the Washans," I began. I wanted my friends to be as aware as I had become of the situation taking place in our world.

I had Barsam's attention immediately. "I have heard rumors, but I never like to give more credence to gossip than I should. Do you think it is more than just tongues wagging, Dyzek?"

Both Camira and Morgayne were listening, even looking at Barsam and me as we spoke, but neither responded to our words right away.

"My parents say that many have run to the foothills of Eloques for personal safety," I continued.

"Yes," Barsam replied. "Do you remember Alagon and his wife and daughter? They left their home just last week. It sits empty, and just this morning I saw one of the Washan visitors looking over their property with great interest."

This news disturbed me greatly. I knew Alagon well, as we all did. He often did business with my father, trading grain for meat on a frequent basis. He was a level-headed man who loved his family very much. He was also very active in local leadership activities. If Alagon had up and fled, things were likely much worse than I understood.

"Well, I can say only this: if my father or mother continue in their concern this deeply, I will act on behalf of all of us," I stated firmly, looking each one of my friends in the eyes, one after another. "We will not be hidden because the standards of the prideful are too high."

Barsam held my eyes, his face grave and his brow knit. "Where you go, I will follow."

I was sixteen lunar years of age then. I am twenty-five now. The road ahead of us was more frightening than any of us could have ever imagined.

Impending Earth

CHAPTER 2

My mother and father used to talk about times before I was given life, times when their parents, and their parents' parents, made lives of their own, with their own bare hands. They would tell me tales, and those tales seemed tall, about those who came before us and how they actually grew their own food and made their own homes. These yarns often seemed so far-fetched since my own parents had established and maintained us with their own strength, and I never gave the stories much credence, but that didn't stop me from sharing them with my friends. When we played, we would even pretend that we were building and growing food, just like in the stories, and just like my own mother and father. It was the way of life in Marmara, and it was peaceful; it was what everyone aspired to in those early days of my life.

In my own time, and even in the time of my parents,

we did not worry about such trivialities anymore. Things changed and improved, and our government did take good care of the people, which allowed many to rest as they got older. Food on Marmara was mass-produced by our 'progressive' government, and they built all of the homes and buildings as well. We lived comfortably enough, but each family's home was designated to hold only a specific number of people; this was how we curbed population growth, which would boom if not regulated.

Food was delivered on a weekly basis, and while it was plentiful, it had to be closely watched so the people would not run out before the next delivery day. This did not allow for much casual snacking, but the food we were provided with was nutritious for the body. When it came to meals and shelter, the Marmaran government took good care of its people.

You see, the government was a 'one-world' rule. There were no sections of law broken down by countries or villages. We had no issues with crime because of the provision made, and violence became virtually unheard-of with the passage of time. One would be tempted to ask why my friends and I no longer live there, but this is a knowledge you will gain soon enough.

All of this became much more controlled, much more drastic, with the arrival of the prideful alien Washans.

Indeed, lives did have many more ups and downs before they came. With their arrival, all things changed, and while many would say it was for the better, it was anything but. The changes they brought carried the illusion of carefree living, but in the end, it reeked of genocide.

I want to begin to tell you of how the segregations started.

As I have clearly stated, our life was good before their arrival. Yes, we worked the land and broke a sweat, but we lived and loved and laughed together. The Washans determined and convinced our governing authorities to establish as well, that some were simply not worthy of this happiness. It would be best for those with less ability to live separately, and the government would care for all of us, completely and entirely. No more physical labor; all you needed to do was contribute the skills you had to the common cause of peaceful survival.

So, with that fact in motion, many of our people became lazy and complacent. Those who held less intelligence than others were utterly dependent on those of us who had more, and the reality was that these people placed a burden on those around them to care for them, not to mention the strains they put on the backs of our government. In retrospect, the entire thing was a carefully orchestrated disaster.

The issue with the arrival of the Washans was how to deal with these 'leeches' accordingly. To rid Marmara of them entirely would provide the Elite of mind and body with a life virtually free of their load, and it didn't take long for the Washans to convince our rulers that elimination needed to take place. But how?

It was not difficult for a plan of action to be slowly, but surely, implemented. Now, in order to have the government care for you so thoroughly, you must have something to offer. This was easy for those who excelled mentally and physically, but for those who were lacking, this was a significant problem. You see, the only real skills possessed by those who were educated involved technology, and on Marmara, we depended on technology for everything by this point. If we wanted an item, all we ever needed to do was…ask.

So this type of training was essential if one wanted to live a fruitful life after the Washans came. They had made all things 'automatic', saying that this would equalize everyone all the more. That was all fine and good, but what about those who were not equipped in this way? What if they were slow of mind and tongue? What if they, the gods forbid, had a physical handicap?

These people were given menial tasks, the jobs no Elite would touch. They were treated like vermin, and they were housed separately from those of the upper echelon. What began as a simple plan to ease the load of those contributing greatly led to a slow, but sure, separation of the people.

I don't think anyone even saw it coming, but in retrospect, I see clearly that the segregations that took place were inevitable.

Before too long, those on the lower crust of our society found themselves wholly shunned by the others, even by their own family and friends. At first, this seemed to work out well for the interests of all involved, even though it did cause an abundant amount of grief and heartache for families whose loved ones were segregated. We all adjusted, believing the final outcome would prove to be the best for all of Marmara. Eventually, things became even worse—much, much worse.

When the segregations first began, they merely started as a designation of tasks. This was fine, of course, because no one wanted to be given a task they could not handle. But, as time passed, the Washans convinced our government that it was antagonistic to our 'goals' to have the Elite and those who were lacking residing together.

Resentments ran rampant, and it got to the point that the Elite practically begged for the others to just be taken out of their hair, and so it was done.

Otherwise, life couldn't have been more perfect. For years I lived with my parents, as did Camira, Barsam, and Morgayne, and we paid hardly any mind to those who were not considered Elite. We were all fortunate to be highly intelligent, useful, and adaptive, and upon reaching full adulthood, we were given our own Elite tasks to fulfill. We were together, and we were happy.

No one was ever sick. Our air was clean and beautiful. Crime was eliminated entirely, and for all intents and purposes the people of Marmara lived and worked in perfect harmony, with the dregs living together off by themselves. The majority of Marmarans, myself included, were initially brainwashed into believing that the best was being done for everyone.

I must admit that I thought life could be no better. I had Camira, who would be my wife, and Barsam had Morgayne. We lived and worked with smiles on our faces. We loved and made love without any care, and we never thought twice about 'needing' anything. All of us became convinced, on one level or another, that the Washans and their grand plans were the salvation of Marmara, even though there was really nothing from which to save us.

But then the 'thinning' began.

After a time it was announced that those with particular, less necessary tasks, would need to relocate. Because of our ages, the four of us were assigned tasks included on this list, and we were required to leave the Elite population as well. No longer would we have it quite so easy. It was no comfort that we were not to live with the dregs; all any of us included could see was that we, too, were being shunned, and we did not understand why.

Almost immediately the prejudice began to show. The Elite would turn up their noses to us just as we had all done to the dregs. We were no good to the Elite because we were not as good as they, yet we were good enough to have our own living section. They hated that we had any skills at all because our existence continued to take something from them that they thought they deserved. With the passage of time, they became more and more hateful and resentful to both us and the dregs.

Dissension was rampant.

I, Dyzek, and my three companions resided together in what was soon tagged section '2 of 2'. We had volunteered to live together in a home with two sleeping quarters, one of which I shared with Camira, the other occupied by Barsam and Morgayne. While we were assigned to live away from the Elite, none of us let it bother our spirits. We lived very peacefully, with great fulfillment and happiness, in love with our mates and content with our lives overall. But soon enough Marmara as we once knew it would become unrecognizable.

This is where I will truly begin to share with you how Barsam, Morgayne, Camira, and I were forced to take control of our own destiny and leave the beauty of our world far behind.

CHAPTER 3

"Camira, I must be going very soon. Are you ready to leave?" I was standing at the table in the food preparation room, ready to leave for my assigned tasks. Camira was always running just a bit behind me, but we always went together. The fact brought a smile to my face.

Her voice resonated from our sleeping quarters. "I will be right out. Be patient, Dyzek! We are never late. You worry too much."

It was early morning, and Barsam and Morgayne were still asleep. I did not worry about waking them because their room was on the other side of our house. It was a good thing because Camira and I could be quite noisy in the morning hours.

Camira appeared before me, looking as fresh as the morning itself. She wore her assigned task clothing, matching pants and shirt in neutral colors. She worked at the food assignment station for the village of Shalbria, programming each family's rations that were to be delivered by the computerized transit system each week. She only needed to be comfortable, so her uniforms sufficed.

I wore the exact same clothing, but in dark blue, like the evening sky. My own daily contributory tasks involved entering information into Marmara's central database regarding the residents of Section 2 and their day-to-day activities. While we both were much more skilled than our jobs required, these mundane tasks were now always assigned to individuals living in 2 of 2.

Camira stood on the tips of her toes and kissed me lightly on my lips. She pulled back and smiled. "I am ready."

Her long black hair was brushed until it was shining. The light glinting off of the silken tresses always caught my eye, and I consistently found myself wanting to run my fingers through it. She was so beautiful.

"Then let's go, before I take you right here!" My statement made her burst out laughing. She was so funny and outgoing; I was truly gifted to have her in my life.

∞

Soon we were standing outside of our house waiting

for our transit. Transportation to those residing in our section was provided by an automatic box rail. There were no seats to get comfortable in; instead, we held onto bars and stood for the entire trip, along with around twenty others from our living section. At first, this segregation bothered us all greatly, but we had adjusted. Now we barely thought twice about it.

After only a few minutes the transit box appeared, and we took our positions inside as it took off for '1 of 2'. This was the 'Elite' section, and it was where all the computers and machines were; they maintained the village of Shalbria and the surrounding areas. If the Elite worked at all, it was at these tasks.

The ride to our tasks was uneventful, as per usual. I always got off the box transit first; Camira would arrive at her destination a couple of minutes after I did. I kissed her goodbye and wished her a prosperous day before stepping out into the sunlight of the day and making my way into the building.

As I made my way to my workstation, I considered the peoples of Marmara. Those of us in '2 of 2' did not have it as easy as the Elite when it came to our day-to-day responsibilities, and we certainly didn't get to enjoy the relaxed life to which they had become accustomed.

No, what we 'lacked' in purity determined that we were the worker bees. To be honest, it wasn't too bad, and it gave us a sense of daily accomplishment if not the feeling of being controlled and our lives dictated to our own details.

Each of the four of us had high levels of intelligence, but we were excluded from the Elite section for a couple of reasons. One: our ages, at the time the initial exclusions that took place were considered when our tasks were assigned, so we were automatically ordered to live in section two. Secondly, each of us had relations that were deemed to be impure. Impurities could consist of anything from sickness to weakness to lack of intellect, and the mere association made us 'lesser' in the eyes of the Elite. It didn't matter that we were of as high quality as they; we had the blood of the impure coursing through our veins, and it would not do to procreate and have further impurities introduced into Marmaran society.

To put it honestly, we were lucky to have what we were given, and we knew it.

I arrived at my station and took my seat, then began preparing for my day. As I organized and adjusted my shared station, one of my co-workers came up behind me.

"Dyzek, have you been keeping up on the recent plans

of the government?" It was the voice of Barrim, a man from my section who frequently obsessed over the goings-on in our world, and even delighted in theorizing that doom was coming to section two in the near future.

I turned in my seat. "I like to think I am aware of what is going on, as you well know. Why? Is there some great news I have missed?"

Barrim shrugged and took a seat in the spare chair next to my desk. He put his elbows on his knees and leaned forward, glancing around conspiratorially. "I have been made aware, by a very dependable source, that the government will announce some critical news before the end of the task week."

"Did you happen to hear what it was all about?", I asked.

He shrugged his shoulders and shook his head. "All I know is that, from what my source said, it will be life-changing for all of the peoples of Marmara."

"Well then, I suppose we will find out soon enough, if it is that vital," I replied.

Barrim stood and stretched out, his arms raised above his head. "I will keep you up to date if I hear anything. You will do the same?"

Now it was my turn to nod, and Barrim left my area

briskly. My curiosity was definitely piqued, and even though I was tempted to putter around to try to learn more from others, I had a pile of work before me. It didn't help that the head of my division was only a couple of doors down. It wouldn't do to be chastised and disciplined for letting my own curiosity get the best of me. I turned my attention to my tasks.

My day passed quickly, much more so than I anticipated. I tidied up my area in preparation for my relief, then packed up my case and headed out to board the transit on time. I was in somewhat of a rush, as my particular transit had been arriving earlier and earlier, or so it seemed. Camira would be in a panic if I was not on it as usual.

I hurried to the appointed location, arriving just as the transit slid into its position. Once on board, I made sure to get a spot with room for my lover, who would be boarding directly. Only a few times had we been separated on the transit, and it always made the trip a bit longer than usual to be apart from her when she was so near to me.

We arrived home safely and quickly to find Morgayne busying herself by putting the pre-prepared food for our evening meal on dishes for all of us to eat. Typically she and Barsam were gone to their own assignments by the time Camira and I got home, so it was a surprise to see her there, not to mention the fact that she was preparing four dishes.

"No tasks for you two this evening, Morgayne?" Camira asked. "Did you both get disciplined for smooching in the supply room?" She laughed at her own joke, which also succeeded in making me smile. The couple had been chastised for this behavior a time or two before, and it always made for a good bit of ribbing when we were in the mood.

Morgayne simply shook her head in response, without looking up from what she was doing. "No," she replied without smiling. "We received word that our area would be shut down for some type of computer analysis."

Barsam and Morgayne both attended tasks at the central computing facility, which was in charge of all computers on Marmara, as well as all transits and other means of travel across the planet. Some of what Barsam did was highly top secret and directly applied to the methods of transportation we used, while Morgayne was involved with high-level record keeping. I wondered what could possibly be going on that would keep them from their tasks; nothing like this had ever occurred before.

Then my good friend entered the room, his hair wet from bathing. Barsam leaned in toward me and shook beads of cooling water onto me from his head. "Well, hello, working man. How were things today?"

"Tasks are tasks, lazy one. How were things here?"

Barsam smiled slyly. "Good, if you like lying in bed naked with a beautiful woman all day. Ideal for a lazy man like me."

Morgayne was bringing the food to the table, and she smiled shyly and blushed. "Barsam, must you?"

"Oh, love. It's all in good fun," he told her, slapping her rear playfully.

I took a bite of a sauce-covered meat-like substance that our government had so courteously provided. After swallowing, I said, "Today, when I first arrived at my tasks, I heard the government would be making a big announcement of some kind before week's end."

Camira's utensil stopped in mid-air before it reached her mouth. "What kind of announcement?"

All of us were sitting down at the table then, and I noticed that the faces of my three friends had suddenly grown serious after I had spoken. "I don't know. What's wrong?"

Morgayne cleared her throat. "The last government announcement put us here, away from everyone," she said quietly. "No government announcements are any good anymore."

"Not to mention the fact that our tasks were canceled for the night," Barsam said. "I wonder if the two facts are somehow related."

I shrugged as I cut my 'meat' into bites. "Hard telling, but who knows. I tried to find out if anyone had any facts, but I had no luck."

"Well," Camira began, "I heard today that further segregation for our section was in the works. It seems the Elite do not even want to hear rumors about us, much less see us for any reason."

Barsam laughed out loud. "We are already about as far away from them as we can get without actually being located in the foothills. How ridiculous! Just a rumor, I am sure."

We all grew still as we ate. My mind, however, was stuck on Camira's words. Was it possible that they were going to make us reside in a third section for simply having relations? What other reason would there be to make another change like this? My stomach was bothered, and I found it difficult to eat.

For the first time in as long as I can remember, we all ate in silence. It seemed I was not the only one turning the day's events and rumors over in my mind. Even Barsam sported a knit brow.

We wrapped up our meal, and each of us took care of inserting our own dishes into the slot to the dish-cleaning unit. Then, still quiet, we all made our way into the sitting room to watch the daily newscast on the large screen the government provided all Marmarans. I sat at one end of the loveseat with Camira snuggling next to me, while Barsam and Morgayne took to the sofa.

The daily evening newscast served two purposes: first, it kept us up-to-date on all the goings-on not only in the village of Shalbria but on the whole of Marmara for the day. Next, it kept us in the loop regarding tasks for the following day. It would let all residents in all sections know if there were any particular problems or other relevant information regarding the areas their tasks were located in, thereby preparing them for the following day's tasks. Another airing took place in the morning hours for those whose tasks required them to work at night.

At first, the evening's announcements seemed quite normal. Most tasks for the following day were going to follow the regular schedule, but those belonging to Barsam and Morgayne would still be canceled the following evening. What was not 'normal' was the fact that they did not tell us why those tasks were canceled.

They just moved onto the next topic, the weather, with smiles on their faces, and I could not help but feel as if the abrupt change of subject was nothing more than a sly distraction.

Within the half-hour, the evening announcements were finished, but rather than find something else on-screen to entertain us all for the evening we all sat in silence for several minutes. After a bit, I glanced around at the faces of my three friends. Everyone looked a bit stumped and confused.

"What do you think, Barsam?" I asked him, a smirk on my face. "Why would they be canceling tasks for the departments you and Morgayne attend?"

He shrugged. A faraway look in his eyes gave away his depth of thought. "All I know is that the only time they even have us step away from our stations is when they need to do a bit of tweaking to the system. They have us leave only so they can enter the appropriate secret passcodes, which we all know are highly restricted," he replied. "I can only assume it could be one of two things: either there is a bug or glitch that needs to be ironed out, or they are conducting restricted business and don't want to risk it being disclosed."

Now Camira sat up straight and leaned toward him.

"What kind of business could it be, Barsam? It doesn't sound right to me."

Barsam only shrugged again, but he knit his brow furiously; he, too, was more than a bit concerned.

"Well," I said as I stood and stretched out my frame, "All we can do is hope it has nothing to do with the rumors of government announcements."

I went into the washroom to take a couple of headache pills. I tended to have a problem with worry at the time, and just listening to the gossip about announcements had given me intense pain. As I was washing the tablets down Barsam appeared in the doorway.

"I didn't want to say it in front of them," he said, gesturing toward the girls in the common area, "but I have a bad feeling in my stomach about all of this. Why would there be rumors of further segregation if they had not started somewhere?"

I reached around behind him and closed the door. Sounds were coming from the screen, and I knew the girls had found something to occupy their evening. "I don't want them upset," I said. "But I agree with you. I think it's time we start trying to find out some details, but we need to keep it between us, okay?"

He nodded, and we both left the bathroom. We all

had family that were Elites, and I had one cousin in particular who had kept me in the mix. His name was Maron, and though I was not permitted to enter his section or even call him, I often ran into him while I was carrying out tasks at work. He was a supervisor and did not mix with section 2 people, but he would make it a point to talk with me if I initiated contact.

Tomorrow I would get Maron's attention. Hopefully, he would be able to give me some information.

Impending Earth

CHAPTER 4

I lay in bed in the darkness that night listening to Camira's soft breathing. We had made love, though to me it had seemed a bit perfunctory, more a distraction from our cares than anything else, the act had managed to bring her quick and comfortable sleep. I was not so fortunate. I lay and turned things over and over in my mind for more than two hours, and the process robbed me of good rest.

As I lay there, I thought about the very first segregation, the one that parted us from those who were now considered the Elite. At the time, we were all pleased and content, and it took all Marmarans by surprise when the government made that first announcement. I remembered it as though it were only yesterday.

∞

"Dyzek!" My mother's voice had rung through the house with its sing-song lilt. "Finish picking up your room quickly now. The evening announcements will begin very shortly!"

I had just been finishing it up anyway, so I simply turned off my light and headed into the common area of my parents' home. There they sat on the sofa, hand in hand, their attention tuned into the screen on the large wall.

I took a seat in a gliding chair and fixed my focus on the screen as well. Maybe Father won't have to work tomorrow, I thought, and we could do a bit of vegetable gathering in the woods together. I loved to spend time with him and was always hopeful his task as a garbage collector would be canceled.

In the initial stages of the broadcast, things were going as usual. Work announcements, governmental news, and expected changes in weather were divulged first; nothing was stated out of the ordinary. The announcer even kept his obligatory smile plastered to his face. So far, nothing wrong here.

But, like a flip of a switch, something was very wrong.

"Tonight, all of Marmara is due to receive some very special news from our reigning government. While the details of the announcement should be expected to cause major changes in all of our lives, it is essential that we all listen closely and abide by the new laws which are being placed over us."

I turned and looked at my parents, they were sporting looks of great concern. The screen and the announcer on it had their complete attention. Now was not the time to ask them what was going on.

The announcer continued. "Here to clarify and provide us with the information we need is Marmara's head governing party, Priest Klantz. Please give Priest Klantz your undivided attention."

The screen went dark for a fraction of a second, but soon it was filled with the image of Priest Myer Klantz. Klantz sat in the highest governing position in our world, and he had a reputation as being a responsible, trustworthy, and stern man. Klantz cleared his throat and fixed his eyes, so they appeared to look straight into the eyes of the watching and waiting public.

"Good evening, brother and sister Marmarans! It is with great pleasure that I address you tonight, though it is accompanied by great trepidation as well," Klantz began. "As all of us are aware, the recent arrival of the Washans has not only brought major changes to our world's style of living, but it has also enlightened us to the variety of ways that our lives can be improved. The Washan people have generously shared with us the successful secrets of their own society, which promise to improve the quality of life on Marmara."

He cleared his throat once more and continued. "While most of us are familiar with the new ideas they have introduced and assisted us to put into practice, the latest is by far the greatest, and I personally believe it will spark the most growth in our communities and on our entire planet."

I looked back over at my mother and father. Their faces had relaxed somewhat, and why shouldn't they? All of us loved and trusted Priest Klantz, even though we really didn't know the Washans. Like me, they believed Klantz had our best interests at heart.

"With that being said," Klantz said, "we will be implementing a plan of community organization that will encourage the growth of our people the way we truly desire. It is essential that the purest of us remain that way, and we must do so without infringing on the rights and liberties of those who are…less pure."

Now my heart began to beat a bit faster. The 'purest' of us? The 'less pure'? What did all of that mean?

"Father, do you under—," I started.

My father jerked his head in my direction. "Quiet!"

I turned my attention back to the screen and Priest Klantz.

"What I am saying is that we have peoples with higher levels of intelligence and skill, and it is imperative that we keep them in an undistracted state," Klantz continued. "Now, this in no way means that any of us are better than another. It just means that we are all in a better situation if we are habituating with those like ourselves. Beneficially contributing parties will be abundantly cared for accordingly, and while all others will have their needs met, it will be in accordance with their contributions only."

"Therefore, beginning tomorrow, directly after the breakfast hour, those who have fewer skills, intelligence, and ability to contribute will be relocated to a second habitat, which is called '2 of 2'." Klantz paused for another moment and glanced at his notes on the podium before him. "There is nothing to be concerned about, though I am aware this sounds both frightening and new. All will continue to have unlimited access to their loved ones, and all will continue in their previously assigned tasks. This will ensure your personal continuity of care by the government."

"During the morning announcements, prior to taking your breakfast, you will be made aware to which section you will be personally assigned. Your determined section will be dependent on the task you hold and the contribution you make. Viewing the morning announcements and receiving your new living assignment is mandatory, and anyone who does not do this will be penalized accordingly."

I looked at my parents then, my eyes wide, but they took no notice of me. They just continued to stare at the screen in silence. None of this sounded good to me, with or without their guidance.

With that Klantz closed the announcements. "I will address all Marmara in the morning, and your assignments will be announced. Be sure to tune in, and have a peaceful night."

The screen went blank, and with that, I began to talk with great insistence. "Father, what do they mean by this? I don't understand what Priest Klantz is saying or doing!"

My father did not feed into my confusion or panic in any way. "I am certain this will in no way affect us, Dyzek."

"Are you sure?" My mother was not convinced.

He did not answer her. "It is time for bed now, son. We will need to rise early for the announcements, but put it out of your mind for the time being."

I stood, my eyes still searching his face, but it gave away nothing. "Bed now, Dyzek."

I turned and stalked off to my room. My father was saying all would be fine, but even then, in the first days of the segregation, I knew that it would not be okay.

I simply did not understand what that meant, but I would find out soon enough.

∞

Now I lay in my bed next to Camira, and the same uneasy feeling filled my stomach. What was going to take place next? How would it affect my friends and me? We had already been relocated once! We contributed to our society and asked for nothing extra. I could not imagine what the announcements would hold for us, nor did I want to.

Tasks were never canceled, and the people did not have problems with attendance due to our excellent health. The fact that cancellations were taking place, and only specific cancellations at that, added up to no good, in my humble opinion. While Barsam and Morgayne's tasks were not top-echelon, they were essential. Who would cover for them? They were explicitly assigned according to knowledge and experience. Even Priest Klantz did not have the ability nor specific knowledge to handle them, and most others did not either.

Something was very, very bad.

I turned over and saw that the sky was beginning to show the sunlight just a bit. I had been tossing and turning all night, and I saw no reason to continue lying there. Not wanting to disturb Camira, who would be able to sleep for a while yet, I quietly rose and donned my robe. I would take my morning beverages and still my spirit.

I made my way into the food preparation area, where I prepared some hot, steaming coffee. I sat at the dining table and waited patiently for it to brew, listening to the bubbling sounds coming from the vessel in which it was prepared. The sounds were comforting if nothing else.

A sound from the common area startled me, and I rose to investigate. Barsam was making his way to the food preparation room and dining area. His coarse black hair was frizzy, standing on end, and this brought a smile to my face.

"You could no longer sleep?" I asked him, grinning at his appearance.

He shook his head, and he did not return my smile. "I haven't slept at all, and don't say anything about my hair."

Barsam poured us both a cup of the morning beverage and brought the vessels over to the table, where he took his regular seat across from mine. "You are considering the cancellations of tasks as well?" he asked.

"How could I not?" I replied. "The inconsistency is enough to wreck my nerves. We all know this is not normal. The slightest deviance from our regular lives takes me back to the segregation."

He nodded and looked out the window at the morning sky. "Yes. It certainly does, doesn't it? I simply can't wrap my mind around what may be hidden up the sleeves of the government, and of the Washans."

We sat in silence, drinking our coffee. There was no need to speak, for we felt each other's apprehension. Hopefully, things would be cleared up during morning announcements. Perhaps it was all nothing, and our minds and hearts would be put at ease.

The two of us chatted on other things for an hour or so; then, we could hear the girls moving around. One of them had turned on the shower, and we knew they would join us shortly. I looked at the timepiece hanging on the food preparation room wall over the dish-cleaning unit; the announcements would begin in just under an hour.

After a short time both girls appeared, and though

they typically bore bright smiles on their faces, they lacked those today. Our home was heavy with the burden of the unknown. None of us trusted our government, not the way we had before the Washans came.

We ate our government-issued breakfasts in silence. I couldn't be sure, but I was convinced we were all pondering the morning announcements. Perhaps they would finally tell us why specific daily tasks were canceled. All we could do was hope. Being kept in the dark made us all afraid and very suspicious.

By the time we were seated comfortably in the living area, the announcements had begun, and they started off on an odd foot indeed. Today, for the first time since any of us could remember, they gave us the weather for all of Marmara first. This took quite a bit of time, and I saw it as a way to ease people, but for what I did not know. Finally, they began announcing task schedules.

"As it was discussed during last evening's announcements, tasks in the transportation, records, and development departments are canceled for the day. All other assignments will carry on as regularly scheduled, and normal attendance to these jobs is expected," the announcer said, the same plastic smile plastered to his face as usual. "There will be an address given by Priest Myer Klantz, which will take place one half-hour prior to evening announcements. Those who are at their work sites will view this from their stations, and viewing is mandatory."

With that, the man on the screen turned to his female counterpart, a red-haired woman with green eyes who stared blankly at the camera with the same smile. He made a joke, and she laughed in an obligatory manner before countering his humor. The jokes signified the end of the morning announcements. I stood and pressed the button to turn off the screen, and I did it forcefully enough to demand the attention of my friends.

"I have only one thing to say about all of this," I began. "I am now convinced, as we all should be, that something we will not like is going to take place." Camira, Barsam, and Morgayne kept their eyes on me, looking to me for guidance. "We will not discuss this outside of the home, or while at our tasks, though I will be attempting to communicate with my distant cousin Maron in an effort to get more information before this evening."

I looked at my friends and took note of the fear in their eyes. Yes, we all knew that it was once again time to brace ourselves. The Washans were up to no good with our government and our people, and it was best for us to be fully prepared.

I continued. "Camira and I will leave for our tasks. You two stay busy and try to maintain your peace. No matter what, the four of us are going to be fine," I said. "We are going to be fine. I will see to it."

My friends nodded at me, and I walked to Camira and took her by the hand. "Grab your jacket, love. It's time for us to leave."

It hurt me to leave Barsam and Morgayne in such an unsure emotional state, but we all knew to continue like the sheep the Washans and Marmaran government wanted us to be.

CHAPTER 5

I expected to arrive at my assignment and see everyone scrambling about, discussing the recent unusual announcements, but nothing like that was taking place at all. Workers sat at their stations carrying out their business as if everything was fine. Had all of Marmara forgotten what had taken place only eight years ago?

I settled in and began to focus on my job, furiously typing away at my keyboard. As time went by, the situation started to fade a bit in my mind, and, before I knew it, the midday meal was being announced. It was time for me to write a message for my cousin Maron and try to get it to him. It would not do to be seen attempting to speak to an Elite during the task day; I would have to exercise caution.

I turned slightly and looked around at my other co-workers, all of whom were rushing to get to the midday meal. They were talking and gabbing amongst themselves, and most of them were smiling and engaging in enthusiastic laughter. No one was paying any attention to me, so I turned back to my desk and jotted a quick note to my cousin, which I would attempt to put in his office without being seen.

Maron,

I realize we cannot speak overtly, but I need to talk to you if possible. Do not agree if it will be detrimental to you in any way.

If you can meet with me, let me know when and where.

Your cousin,

Dyzek

I folded the small sheet until it was nothing more than a small square sitting in the palm of my hand. It would be easy enough to keep out of sight if someone were to confront me. I then stood and walked into the main corridor which ran amongst all the workstations. I looked around carefully. Not a soul was in sight.

I crossed the work area, walking briskly and keeping my head down. When I reached Maron's station, I was pleased that he had left his door wide open, and I was easily able to place the note directly on the keyboard to his computer. I then left the room and began to walk to the dining room, but I had taken no more than ten steps when I was startled by a stern voice behind me.

"You there!"

I turned on my heel, jumping slightly. "Yes?" My heart was pounding in my chest.

It was a short, brown-haired man with freckles on his cheeks. The sunlight had been generous to him. "I just began in this division, and I can't remember how to get to the midday meal. Could you take me?"

It took all I had in me to keep from breathing aloud with relief. I smiled at the small man. "Of course. It can be hard to take in so much in such a short period of time. Follow me. I'm Dyzek."

He approached me holding out his hand in greeting. "I am Syman. Thank you for your assistance. I am much more nervous than I thought I would be."

I shook his hand. He could be no more nervous than I. "Don't be. You will have the hang of things around here in no time."

The tension drained from my body, and I escorted Syman, the new task-hand, for his meal.

∞

My task day was nearly over, and I had not been nearly as productive as I would have liked to have been. If anyone was paying attention, they would be suspicious of my behavior based only on the lack of work I had done. I was one of the top workers in my division because of my high numbers and the high quality of my work, but one would not have guessed it based on my contributions that day.

I was staring at my small screen, my hands on my keyboard, but I was entering nothing. I could not get my mind off the unknown, and it was beginning to get on my nerves. I had to snap out of this or I was going to get myself into trouble. They watched us like hawks when it came to the work we contributed, especially those of us who resided in '2 of 2'.

Suddenly my cousin Maron's voice, low and discreet, came over the small speaker at my station. It was hardly more than a whisper, but I nearly jumped out of my skin anyway.

"Dyzek, it is Maron. I will be in the supply closet in two minutes. It will be locked. Tap on it, and make sure no one sees you."

That was all he said, and I didn't dare risk answering him. I rose and looked around nervously. No one was paying me any mind at all.

Soon I was strolling before the closet, looking around to see if anyone was watching me. If anyone was, I could not see them, so as soon as I reached the door, I tapped twice on it, very lightly. It flew open immediately. Maron had hold of my arm in seconds and pulled me inside. He shut the door quickly and secured it with a sliding bolt that seemed to serve no practical purpose on the inside of the door.

"We have only a moment," Maron began. "What do you need?"

I cleared my throat nervously. "Why are tasks being canceled? Do you know, Maron?"

"You know I cannot discuss this with '2 of 2' segregates, Dyzek."

Now I looked at him, my eyes stern. "Less pure or not, we are family, and I have no one else. Something is wrong; what is it?"

Maron's eyes shifted nervously. "If you tell anyone you heard this from me, I will deny it, and you will be severely penalized, Dyzek."

"Of course," I said quietly.

He looked at the floor and shifted his weight from one foot to the other. "Tasks in certain divisions were canceled in order for additional programming to be completed in those areas."

"But why?"

Now he shook his head in frustration. I could tell that he was struggling within himself about whether to divulge what he knew to be highly classified. Finally, he got a look of resignation on his face and said what I already knew in my soul.

"They are adding a third section that will house a lower level of segregates," he whispered. "Those who do not contribute. The filthy and sick, the ugly and weak. They are to be labeled the 'Dregs', and they will be housed at the Eloques foothills."

I could not even breathe. What all of us had dreaded was becoming a reality. The government plans to separate us even further. They were going to minimize our numbers until there was nothing we could say or do about any of the decisions being made.

He continued. "It will be referred to as '3 of 3'."

I closed my eyes and tried to clear my scrambled brain. "Who will be sent?"

"Only the worst of the worst," he replied as he took hold of the sliding bolt. "I must go; I can tell you no more. Tune into announcements this evening for more. Do not leave this room for five full minutes, and lock the bolt after I leave."

With that my cousin Maron was gone, and I was left alone with my panic and despair.

I could feel the salty drops of tears welling up behind my eyes, and it burned. I would not cry, for there was no time for such foolishness. But what would I do? I slowed my breathing down with discipline and focused my mind on solid thought.

I would finish my tasks for the day. I would then catch the transport and remain calm before Camira until we reached '2 of 2' (or was it '2 of 3'?) where we could talk without fear. I had to be the strong one; I had to be stable. But it seemed that the world was crashing down around my ears. Please, understand, I was not the only one who would be concerned about this! Everyone in '2 of 2' would be petrified. All of us had gone through segregation before, with the exception of those born after the fact, and the memory would never leave us. Now I found out with certainty that history would repeat itself. My stomach was sick.

Again, there had been others, families, who had taken to the foothills to evade separation. I had never been there myself, and the people were not permitted to venture there legally, but I had heard tales. If they were in any way close to true, then the living conditions for the Dregs would be terrible. The fine umbrella of care the government provided the Elite, and the 'Mids' in '2 of 2' (as we were sometimes called, with tones of dishonor) would not be extended to protect them from the proverbial rains. I realized they were being referred to as 'Dregs' with full intent.

I stood up straight and took a deep breath, then ran my hand through my hair and wiped my eyes. After placing my ear against the inside of the closet door, I listened to the sounds coming from the workstations on the other side; everything sounded normal, so I gently drew the bolt and opened the door.

It was like going from a darkened room directly into the sun. Everything was brighter, more alive, but nothing was the same. I saw all of the people, a vast majority of them Mids like myself, going about their tasks. None of them bore a look of contentment or solitude. Brows were knit all around, and smiles didn't exist there. The truth was everyone was very, very concerned about what Priest Klantz would be saying during the announcements that evening.

By the time I got back to my workstation, there was only about an hour left to focus on tasks, and that was what I did, to the best of my ability, anyway. As I have said, it wouldn't do to appear suspicious due to lack of productivity. Fortunately, the hour passed quickly, and I was able to wrap things up and head home. I needed to talk to my friends and tell them what I knew.

∞

Camira and I did not speak on the trip to '2 of 2' outside of greeting each other and smiling. More than once I caught her looking at me, trying to read my face. She knew that I had planned to speak to Maron today, and I knew that she was anxious to find out if I had been able to, and, if so, what he had said. I didn't want to start any conversation concerning the issue while in the presence of others, so I would directly respond to her searching looks with a smile, and it seemed to appease her at the time.

Barsam and Morgayne were playing music on the sound system when we walked in the door, and to me, it seemed to present a false sense of stability and tranquility. I was pleased that it was on, though. They were smiling with oblivion. To see them thoroughly happy for the first time in two days was satisfying to me, for I didn't know when the next time we would be truly happy, if ever.

When we entered, Barsam immediately rose from his

place in the common area and lowered the music. "How was your day, you two?"

Camira smiled at him. "Mine was fine. There seemed to be a bit of tension at my work site today, but no one spoke of anything out of the ordinary." She turned to me, then, she hung her jacket on one of the hooks by the door. "What about you, Dyzek? Were you able to glean any information from Maron?"

I nodded without speaking and hung my jacket next to hers. "We should sit at the meal table to talk," I said lightly. I didn't want to stir anyone's emotions up before I had to, but my tone did nothing to help my goal. All of them knew that talking meant I had some news to deliver, and their faces became immediately shadowed.

We sat while Camira poured glasses of ice water for us to drink. Once she had taken her seat, I began.

"I indeed spoke to Maron today," I began. "I am afraid what I have to report is far less than ideal."

Barsam gave me his rapt attention. "What did he say?"

I decided to lay it on the table without any stalling or side-stepping. "The government is announcing the opening of another segregated section at the Eloques foothills."

The room fell quiet right away as my companions processed what I had just said. Finally, Morgayne spoke.

"What does that mean?"

I shrugged slightly, then shook my head. "It means they intend to separate another group of people from this section. Maron said this group is referred to as 'Dregs', and they will be considered even lesser than we are." I looked at each one of my friends. "There will be more segregations, and those taken will not be cared for, as they are lesser contributors."

Camira stood, anger across her face. "How can they separate us further? Haven't they differentiated enough?"

"Obviously not," I replied simply.

Now Barsam spoke. "How will they determine who will be taken?"

"According to Maron it will be the sickliest, the ugliest, and those most lacking in intelligence," I said. "To me, that means all who depend on us and the Elite currently in any way without pulling their own weight."

I continued. "When we tune into announcements after the evening meal, we will find out the details. What I am sure of is that the tasks that were canceled were canceled so they could complete programming for the new sector. Like transportation and segregation data input. It's that simple."

We all sat in silence now. I had been able to process

the information in the hour at the office, though not completely, but my friends were still in a state of shock.

"What if they separate us?" Morgayne said, her voice cracking. She had a good point, and it was the same thing I was concerned about. The fact was that we were considered less than the Elite, but we were all still contributors. But all of us knew that Morgayne herself was the most timid and the least skilled of us all. If they could manage daily tasks without my friends' attendance, the government might say it didn't need them, and since they would not be contributing, they would be relocated. We had to be prepared.

I was compelled to reassure these people whom I considered my family. "I do not believe that will happen, Morgayne, and if it does, we will resist. I promise you, we will not let anybody be taken from our home.

"Announcements are scheduled to begin thirty minutes earlier than usual to allow time for Priest Klantz to address the sectors." I looked at the clock on the wall. "We have an hour to eat, or we can talk about what we should do."

Camira stood, her eyes flashing. "Who can eat at a time like this? It is a given that we will determine what should be done should they attempt to separate us in any way! Get it together, Dyzek! Food is not the priority right now!"

I nodded. I knew that would be the response from all three of my friends, and the other two were clearly nodding in agreement as well. "It's settled then," I said. "No one will be taken. If by chance, one or more is ordered to the foothills without the others, we will bar no holds to protect and hide them from the government, and the dirty Washans as well. Unless we all are ordered to be sent to the foothills together. In that case, we will not resist. Agreed?"

All three of them spoke at once in response. "Agreed!"

We all fell into contemplative silence once again. After about ten minutes I looked up at my comrades and broke that silence. "It will be called '3 of 3'."

"'3 of 3'," Camira spat angrily. "Ridiculous! They want nothing more than to be rid of those of us they see as a burden, and this will assist them in weakening the people by diminishing their numbers. It is no more than that, and it is no less."

"Yes," I said. It was all I could think of to say.

Finally, we all stood and made our way into the common area. It was early, but we all wanted to be mentally prepared for whatever our government decided to spring on us now, for we knew full well that none of it was right in any way. It was time to buck up and be ready for anything.

CHAPTER 6

"Good evening, all of Marmara! I, Myer Klantz, and the entirety of your government hope this address finds you healthy, happy, and well-provided-for by our efforts," the Marmaran priest began, a broad smile on his face that did not touch his brown eyes. "Thank you for cooperating by tuning into the evening's announcements a bit early tonight. We extend gratitude for your attendance."

We sat in our seats, Camira next to me and Morgayne by Barsam, and we stared at the screen without speaking to or looking at each other. Priest Klantz had our rapt attention, and nothing could distract our nervous hearts at this point.

He continued. "As you may well have assumed by now, our governing authorities have been in the process of implementing some changes that will prove to be instrumental in increasing the happiness, comfort, and contentment of all the peoples in both sectors one and two. While we are sure you are experiencing some apprehension at what these changes will mean to you and the lives you are now living, I want to personally reassure you that each and every one of you will benefit greatly from them, just as you did the first time we implemented change."

Now I turned to my companions and sought out their faces, but none of them noticed my glances. I turned my attention back to Klantz. My stomach was churning, and my hands were shaking; I was terribly nervous.

"Have no fear, dear citizens, for we have only your very best interests at heart at all times. It is imperative to us that your living arrangements prove to benefit your needs, and your contributions to Marmara, in the best, most thorough way possible," he continued. "With that being said, it is the opinion of the Marmaran government, based on proven advice and the guidance of the Washan people, that a third sector would greatly improve the services we provide our citizens, as well as help them to make the most successful personal and professional contributions possible."

I heard Morgayne take a sharp breath, and I turned in her direction. I could see her eyes tearing over in the light of the screen. I then turned to Camira. She looked furious, and once again did not notice my look.

Klantz then said, "For the last several weeks we have been preparing more than adequate living quarters near the Eloques foothills for individuals who will be relocating there. This sector, '3 of 3', will house some of you who are unable to contribute as you would like. We have adjusted all transportation and provision with the computers in accordance with the needs of this group, and they, too, will be wonderfully provided for and cared for by our government.

"No more will they need to worry that they are unable to contribute. These individuals can finally relax without feeling 'less than' or inadequate, and those who reside in '1 of 3' and '2 of 3' will be able to continue their day-to-day lives without concern for their less able loved ones. Those in '3 of 3' will be able to finally settle down and begin families that are entirely covered by the shelter of their government without the burden of downward glances and stares. They will finally be complete."

Barsam stood. He was enraged and shaking. "Dictator!" he screamed at the screen.

"Barsam, sit!" I said sternly, and he responded immediately by sitting, his fists clenched in his lap.

Klantz went on. "Over the next month, three days a week, during the evening announcements, names of those chosen to relocate will be announced. They will be announced during the first, third, and fifth day of the task week. If your name is announced, you will have one week to comply by gathering your possessions and reporting to the assigned transport to be taken to Eloques. Only current sector two residents will be moved."

Now the priest got a concerned look on his face. "While this news may be frightening for those of you in '2 of 2', I implore you to cooperate fully to further the bettering of Marmara, both for your benefit and the benefit of all our peoples. If any attempt to avoid transport is made, there will be severe penalties, both for the offenders and anyone assisting them."

Now he cleared his throat and looked down at his podium, breaking 'eye contact' with the viewers for the first time. He paused, cleared his throat again, and finally said, "Thank you for tuning in as ordered. We look forward to serving you all in your new homes, and we look forward to the flourishing future of all Marmara." With that, he smiled, nodded curtly, and abruptly walked away from the podium.

The screen went black for a fraction of a second, then a worded message appeared. "Please enjoy a fifteen-minute intermission, after which regular evening announcements will commence…"

I immediately braced myself for the outbursts of my companions, but all of us sat in silence, and to me, it seemed to last forever. Morgayne was the first to speak, much to my surprise, and what she said broke my heart.

"I will be one of them, you know," she said quietly.

Barsam was on his feet once again. "Never! You are a contributor, and they need you! Don't even think that way!"

Morgayne's hand gently touched his leg in an effort to calm him. "Barsam, my job is the least important contribution of the four of us. The numbers he gave dictate that at least one will be taken from every home."

"Never!" he screamed yet again. He began to pace back and forth across the room, his eyes wild and roaming as he thought. Camira and I remained still. Finally, he looked to me, a defeated look on his face. All of us knew in our hearts that Morgayne was very likely correct in her assumption.

Not only was her task considered 'less important', but her heritage was also one of poor health and weak eyes. She was smaller and weaker than most, and twice this year she'd had to receive medical attention for ailments.

Barsam spoke. "Dyzek?"

I met his eyes, offering comfort with my own, but my mind was going a thousand miles an hour. I glanced at both Morgayne and Camira as well. All three of them looked to me in silence.

Finally, I spoke directly to Barsam. "We will let no one in this house be relocated, and we will go to any extreme we are forced to go to in efforts to ensure this," I said. "I will go to the death to keep our family together."

All fell quiet once again, then Barsam spoke to me again. "Do you swear, my brother?"

"With my entire being, my brother."

Now Camira spoke. "We need a plan, in case we have to take action."

I nodded. "Yes, and we will begin to discuss that plan tomorrow after tasks. We must watch announcements; I am sure all of us will have tasks, which will mean the two of you will work tonight. I will think on all of this. Have no fear, anyone. We will all be fine."

But I just wasn't so sure.

∞

Camira and I lay in bed that night in the dark, our home deathly quiet. Just as I had thought, both Morgayne's and Barsam's tasks had resumed, and with little rest, they had been forced to leave for them shortly after the announcements had concluded. Now I lay next to my companion, both of us awake and very contemplative.

We lay in silence, Camira's head resting on my shoulder, my arm around her, holding her close. Her tapered fingertips trailed up and down over my chest, but I hardly felt it; I simply had far too much on my mind. I had to figure out a solid course of action for protecting my family if it was required of me, and deep inside I knew that it would be.

I continued to turn things over and over in my head for some time, and Camira's fingers seemed to keep time for my thoughts. If any of our names were announced for relocation during the next month, we would have very few choices in terms of courses of action. Running to the foothills had been the preferred method of escape during the initial segregations. What had the government done with all of those who had defied that first order? They had to have done something in order to build new quarters and ready it for living. Perhaps they had been shown mercy and were being allowed to remain there. The thought was foolish; since the Washans came, defiance was viewed not only as a crime but as a major weakness of character as well.

I was sure they had been put to death.

I did not see running with my friends as a good option, not without refuge ready and waiting. The foothills had been the last safe place on Marmara since the segregations began, and now that was taken over as well. Marmara was a tiny planet; with the new sector in the foothills, it would be occupied in its entirety.

Could we successfully hide the person or persons who were chosen? This had been attempted on many levels and was never successful. But I happened to believe that nothing was impossible with proper preparation and planning. With more thought and conference with my companions, we might be able to come up with an answer that involved putting someone under the radar, but for how long?

"What are you thinking, Dyzek?" Camira's voice pulled me from my thoughts, and in acknowledgment, I began to gently stroke her long black hair.

"I am contemplating our options, just in case," I replied.

She flattened her palm on my chest, and I felt her nod her head slightly. "Yes. I believe a plan will be needed. I think Morgayne may be right in her fears."

"I do as well."

She propped herself up on her elbow and looked down at me through the darkness. "What can we do?"

"Well," I began, "we really have only a couple of choices: hide or run. I don't know where we would run to, with the taking of the foothills. It is my initial thought that Barsam and I should spend one of our break days, or nights, should I say, to venture to the foothills and see what has taken place there."

"How will that help? The foothills have been taken," she said.

"Yes," I replied, "But how much of them? I have never been there, and for all we know there are nooks and crannies that have not been noticed by our government. I want to see what has happened to those who absconded there the first time around."

Camira laid her head back down. "I am sure they are all dead."

"Yes. But it will help us to know if there is a place near the foothills or beyond where we could take cover in the case of an emergency. You know, somewhere where the ones being ordered to segregate could basically hide right under their noses."

She let out a sigh. "That sounds very off-the-cuff to me, Dyzek."

"Yes, but I need more time to think."

Our discussion ceased at that point, and Camira's fingers began to stroke my chest again. Yes, Barsam and I would steal away at the end of this week, and we would investigate the foothills. For all I knew, they took over only a small portion. Maybe they didn't even find any of the runners who had taken refuge there. Maybe there was still someplace safe for us to hide if we needed to.

I tried to push the issue out of my mind. Camira's soft fingertips began to travel lower and lower, and soon they were brushing against my crotch. I began to grow hard instantly, and suddenly the impending segregations were the last thing on my mind. She stroked me gently, and I grew, and after only a moment she slid down the bed and stole under the covers. In seconds I was in her mouth in full. I closed my eyes and concentrated on her warm tongue and soft lips. I focused on her steady hand and its caresses.

"Oh, Camira. I needed this," I whispered.

She only groaned in response, and I grew rock-hard from the sound of her voice. She felt it and picked up the pace instantly. She knew just what to do for me, and in a matter of only seconds, I let go in her mouth. She kept me there, stroking me until I was spent and could bear it no more, and I cried out from the pleasure.

She pulled away and lay next to me on her pillow, listening to me pant and waited for me to gain my sanity again.

"There. Now you should be able to think more clearly," Camira told me, and I could hear that she was smiling. "Wake me when you come up with your genius plan, darling." She gave me a quick kiss on the cheek and rolled over to sleep, and within minutes her breathing settled, and she was dreaming.

Impending Earth

CHAPTER 7

I woke to the sound of the main door of our quarters being closed and the hushed voices of Barsam and Morgayne as they returned from their tasks. They always tried to be quiet, but the two were not adept at stealth by any means. I smiled and carefully put my feet on the floor so as to not wake my love; she could get another couple of hours of sleep if I let her.

I donned my night robe and made my way from the darkness of the bedroom and into the light of the food preparation room. The sun would not rise for another hour, making the light essential. My friends sat at their places at our meal table, both with plates of food that Camira had readied for them before we retired.

"Good morning," I said, smiling. "How were tasks?"

Barsam looked up at me but did not return my smile. "Fine, fine," he replied, turning his attention back to his food.

"Everything was good," Morgayne responded, and she did smile. "I am trying to keep my spirits and hopes up. How was your night?"

"Uneventful, and I found it a bit hard to sleep, though Camira fell asleep easily enough."

Morgayne stood and placed her plate in the dish cleansing unit. "I think I am going to turn in. I am a bit exhausted from all of the stress and anxiety."

"Yes," I replied. "You should get some rest."

She smiled at me, then bent over to Barsam and kissed him before making her way down the hall to their room. Once I heard their bedroom door close, I sat at the table with my friend. "How are you holding up, brother?"

He took a drink of water to cleanse his palate. "As well as can be expected, I suppose. I can't stop thinking about the segregations. I have the same sense of dread that Morgayne expressed. I hate to say this and give voice to it at all, but I fear she is right. She is what the government would call one of the 'weaker links'."

I nodded. "I have been thinking things over all night, and all we can do is plan and take things as they come. But I do think that you and I should take one of our nights off and visit the foothills, Barsam."

He looked up at me. "Why? What good would that do?"

"Well," I began, "we would be able to see if there are any people who survived, and we could investigate possible hiding places, just in case."

He thought this over for a moment. "Yes, that is wise. We need to know our options."

"I see it this way," I said. "If nothing else it will give us perspective on how they handled the insurgents from the first segregation. If they are living in the new quarters, perhaps they can give us details about the area. Are there caves? Where did they hide?"

"But if they are dead, and the place is barren until the relocations, we may be able to explore and find out for ourselves, unnoticed."

"We will hide if we find a place?" he asked.

I shrugged. "I don't really know yet, Barsam. I am taking things a step at a time. My heart is just telling me this is a good first step if nothing else."

"I am with you wherever you go, Dyzek," he swore to me. "You know this."

I nodded solemnly. "If anyone of us is to be segregated, we will all react to protect the other, no matter what."

"No matter what…"

Camira and I left home for our tasks a couple of hours later. Before we left, we had a short conference with Barsam and decided we would not discuss the segregations at all, with anyone, when outside of our home. We would appear to be fully content and cooperative at all times. We would behave the way the Elite acted when we were taken.

∞

I arrived at my task site with a smile on my face and pep in my step, as false as it was. I spoke to all who talked to me, and I kept my tone friendly. On two occasions others tried to engage me in conversation regarding the previous night's announcements, and both times I was able to successfully escape their attempts. Regardless, my mind was fixed on the segregations, and I was filled with preoccupied concern.

With that being said, my production that day was exceedingly high, with all things considered, and when the day drew to a close, I was even pulled aside by a monitoring supervisor from the Elite section and told how valued my work was at the site. I knew then that my name would not be announced during the separation calls, and while this helped my heart to rest easy, it did nothing for the worry I felt regarding my companions.

I fretted terribly inside and visualized all scenarios over and over in my head, obsessing. What if Camira were called? I would kill anyone who tried to take her from me, and I would accept any penalty with great pleasure. Barsam? Morgayne? The same. I would rather die than allow the only family I had to be taken. Anyone who attempted it would die trying, and I swore this to myself silently.

I fantasized about how I would drive a knife through their chests, or bash their skulls in with a club. I planned out strategic attacks in my mind, trying with futility to protect people who, as of yet, had not been threatened. It was only one day after the announcement, and I was beginning to feel like a genuine madman.

I would go home and place weapons behind every door and next to our beds. I would fashion locks on our lockless doors. I would design booby traps that would do great bodily harm to anyone who tried to cross our threshold. I would keep my family safe.

I was determined, and I would succeed.

Impending Earth

CHAPTER 8

The foothills of the Eloques Mountains were not as one may visualize the foothills on a plush and fertile green planet like Marmara to be. Rather than being plush with vegetation, these foothills consisted of rolling hills of dark red dirt and sand, mostly packed very hard. As I have said, I have never been to the foothills personally, but learning the geography of Marmara thoroughly was a requirement when we were educated as youth.

There was no modern lighting provision in the past; I knew that for a fact. It was deserted prior to the runners of the first segregation, and even with the new encampment being built, I wasn't sure if there would be modern lighting now. To visit there at night, we would have to virtually travel in the darkness, and on foot, if we wanted to go unnoticed.

∞

Barsam and I left late that night, out my bedroom window. Our home was situated on the very outskirts of '2 of 2', now '2 of 3', and stealing away would be easy for us if we were careful. Each of us carried a small pocket light for emergencies but did not use it. The final moon, Fortitus, was shining brightly high in the sky to the west, while its predecessor, Magnus, was just starting to reach the far-east horizon. We had plenty of light to show us the way.

We wore our darkest clothing and cloaks, and the women fashioned longer head-coverings to streamline our profiles in the night. If anyone took notice of our travels at any point, we would drop quickly to the ground and pray that they lost sight of us in the darkness. They also packed two sling-type bags for us to carry. Inside they gave us sandwiches and containers of drinking water and crackers. They also gave us an emergency change of clothing, if needed, and various implements and small tools for use in an emergency. This was going to be risky any way you looked at it, but it had to be done, and it helped to be as prepared as possible. They also packed a knife for each of us, for protection.

We walked in silence and paid close attention to our surroundings at all times. The foothills were a good five spans from '2 of 3', so we were in for traveling all night. I remember having to run spans in mid education. It would not pay off to allow ourselves to be discovered by making small talk, no matter how tedious the journey.

After we had been walking for nearly a full hour and had not encountered anyone, not even a sound, I turned to Barsam and whispered, "So far, so good. I expected to at least see foot-guards or street supervisors by now."

Street supervisors were appointed government patrollers that monitored the streets of '2 of 3' on a constant basis. This was to ensure that no Mid made their way into the Elite sector and disrupted their purity or lifestyle in any way. The supervisors were not known for violence, but they upheld the order with strong assertiveness if necessary.

Barsam whispered back, "I noticed. We can only hope to have so much luck the entire journey."

We continued on, speaking to each other only when one of us thought we heard something. This happened a number of times, but each time proved to be a false alarm. The night would remain still as we stopped to listen, and there was never any movement or lights that appeared. The closer we got to the actual foothills the more convinced we became that our own nerves were playing tricks on us.

Finally, after what seemed like forever, the terrain began to change, subtly at first, then eventually the hills became very apparent, both underfoot and on the horizon.

"We are very close now," Barsam said in a low voice.

"Yes," I replied. "Keep your eyes peeled. Do you see any lights, even in the distance?"

We stopped yet again and observed everything around us, straining our eyes in the darkness. After a moment Barsam spoke. "I see nothing, Dyzek. I do not even see any lights coming from between the hills."

"The night stays consistent all around," I said, a bit of incredulity in my voice. "I think we should continue on in the same straight direction; it is here, and we know it is."

"Perhaps they have it shut down?" Barsam questioned.

I began walking again. "I'm not sure, but we need to be cautious. Let's keep moving."

We continued on the same path, growing quiet again and continuing to scan the skyline as best as we could at that hour. The sky was navy blue, and the ground that met it was just a couple of shades darker. It was important to pay very close attention. Even if the new encampment wasn't lit in some way, there would surely be guards or supervisors of some kind watching the place, but how could we know the current state of '3 of 3'?

We climbed and descended the next two hills, both of which reached taller and higher than those before it. We were definitely getting closer to the heart of things now, and my heart began to beat a little faster. There was still no light to give away any specific location, even reflecting in the distance in the night sky; there was nothing. Suddenly, as we crested the second hill since stopping, I saw in the darkness a massive grouping of dark squares in the distance, right at the foot of the hill, about a half a span away. The squares were too uniform to be natural; they were man-made and placed there intentionally.

I stopped and held my arm out to stop Barsam, all the while straining my eyes in the darkness. "There it is."

He stopped short. "Where? Oh!"

A valley, nestled deep into the hills, about two spans from the main mountain range, sat peacefully below. Not a flicker of light nor a sound emitted from the valley, which was filled with four long rows of six black squares apiece: tents. Twenty-four in all. At the rear of the rows was a sizeable rectangular tent, the same color, and it ran the width of the rows. I assumed this was for staff and services for the people who would live here.

Neither of us spoke; for some time we merely stared at our discovery. '3 of 3', designed and constructed for the 'Dregs', consisted of nothing but a group of tents.

"Do you hear anything at all?" I whispered to Barsam.

He was still for a moment, then shook his head. "Nothing."

I turned to him. "Let's go in."

He nodded once curtly, and both of us advanced, but not too quickly. We continued to tread lightly and listen carefully, but as we approached, the only sounds we could hear were an occasional bird and the breeze. After only a few minutes, we came to the corner of a large metal fence, and there we stopped to listen and look some more.

We then began to crawl the perimeter of the fence, very slowly, on our hands and knees. We would go about two yards, then stop, listen, and look. We did this for nearly an hour, uneventfully, and then finally came to a gate in the enclosure, closed and locked, of course. We quietly began to inspect the gate as best we could, but it was too difficult to see, and the night in the valley was very dark; I could not believe there was no one around watching the place.

The only thing we could clearly see was a large white

sign with black lettering. It was securely fastened to the main gate, and it read as follows:

Attention:

Per the order of the Marmaran government, in cooperation with the Washan government, entry is prohibited for any non-resident into this sector.

Sector '3 of 3'

NO UNAPPROVED ENTRY OR EXIT.

PROCEED AT RISK OF

SEVERE PENALTY.

I read the sign twice, with Barsam reading by my side. Finally, I turned to him and said, "The Dregs will be prisoners, my brother."

Barsam remained silent.

I allowed him to finish processing the contents of the sign, then I touched his arm to pull him out of his angry trance.

"Barsam, come now. Follow me to the corner of the fence. Perhaps the girls packed something we can dig under with, or cut the metal with," I whispered.

"Yes," he replied, his eyes glued to the sign. "Let's go."

We ran back to the first corner of the fence we had approached upon arrival. There we knelt to the ground, and, using my portable light source, I began to rummage through my bag. Barsam proceeded to do the same.

I found nothing that would even come close to cutting into the metal fence. No small saws or snips of any kind. I did locate a small multiple-use tool with a pretty hefty file, but I knew it would not do the trick, not in a million years. The only other thing was a large serving spoon at the bottom of my sling bag.

"I have nothing but a spoon and a variety tool!" I spat with disgust. "What about you?"

Barsam turned to me and smiled. "Did Camira pack your bag?" he asked.

"Yes, and Morgayne packed yours. Why?"

"You won't believe this," he said, his smile growing. He pulled his hand from his sling, his grip tight around a pair of large bolt-cutting snips.

I closed my eyes and let out a huge breath, along with a small laugh. "Thank the gods for Morgayne."

"Indeed," Barsam said smugly.

We knelt down next to the fencing, Barsam with the snips and me holding my small light down inside of my bag. I formed a cave-type shape with the sling's pouch in an effort to direct the tiny stream of light out of the bag so we wouldn't have to risk shining it directly and being discovered. It worked sufficiently, though we could see only a tiny portion of fencing at a time.

It was a silver metal, an aluminum-type. There were thicker bars which formed perfect squares of approximately three square inches apiece. More narrow metal bars filled each square, five of them horizontally and five vertically, making the fencing resemble mesh.

"Will the snips fit between the bars?" I asked.

He nodded. "If we begin with one of the thicker ones, toward the bottom. It is going to be a long, time-consuming job, from the looks of it."

"Well, we have no other choice," I replied.

Barsam put the tool down and turned to me in full. "Dyzek, what if we are doing this for nothing? And what if we are then caught, for nothing?"

"What do you mean?"

"Well," he began, "We do all this, and we get caught, or we don't, and we take this massive risk, then no one in our family is segregated. Do we risk too much?"

"Barsam, for the sake of the future, it is a risk I am prepared and willing to take."

He looked at me, staring at my eyes in the dark night, for a long moment. Finally, he nodded with resignation.

"Yes. It is better to prepare for the worst than to not prepare at all."

We both turned back to the fence, and I refocused the light. Barsam jiggled and manipulated the head of the snips, forcing them into a tight gap at the bottom that was wider than all the rest. He got hold of the thick wire and pressed the grips together forcefully and quickly.

Snap!

The sound seemed amplified a million times, and I was sure we had stirred everyone on the whole of Marmara. We both held a sharp breath and began to look around furiously. We were silent for a long moment, and finally, we both exhaled very slowly.

Not a sound. Nothing. There was no one here, and if they were, they were deaf or fast asleep.

He worked his finger into the gap and attempted to bend the metal he had cut out and away. I did not think it was even worth trying, but he grasped it between his gloved fingers and pulled it toward him with all his might. Slowly but surely it gave and bent out and away from the fence.

"Was it difficult?" I asked.

He looked at me and shook his head, his eyes wide with wonder. "It was amazingly…easy."

So he focused on clipping, making a single cut about

every other minute, giving us time to listen between clips. After about a half-hour, his hands began to ache and freeze up, and we exchanged tasks for a while.

During my shift the sun began to light the sky, approaching from the west. We were positioned next to a large, dry bush. It was very full in body, and I thought it would serve as a good covering. By the time we switched tasks again, the sky was well-lit, and we stopped briefly to look around in the light and see what we could see.

The tents were large and black, and they looked to be constructed of an excellently solid and sturdy material. The shelter closest to us appeared to have a single large flap in the front, serving as the main door, I assumed. There were smaller flaps, all fastened shut with metal clamps, in the middle of the tent walls all around each structure: windows.

There was no grass. The ground was hard, red dirt. There were two chairs on each side of the main door of each tent in my sight, and they, too, appeared to be constructed of the same material as the tents. Alongside each structure were two poles, each about ten feet from each other, and they had two durable-looking white cords running between them. My mother used similar poles and cord to hang drying clothing on when I was a small child, but now we all used machines.

The Dregs would be washing their clothes by hand.

"I think it is vacant," Barsam said.

I nodded. "It appears that way. The segregations begin the day after tomorrow during evening announcements. Guards will likely arrive to make preparations for transports that morning, during the beginning of the normal task week."

I thought twice. "We will keep quiet, though, in case residents are here and still asleep. I would think they would be up if they here, though."

We turned our attention back to the fence. We were cutting a half-oval, large enough for either of us to crawl through. We had it half done. Two more shifts and we would be through. We had been at it nearly two-and-a-half hours, and I guessed it was about the eighth hour of the morning, just barely. I supposed we would be done by the eleventh hour at the latest if we did succeed in gaining entry.

Barsam began once again, and during this round he made progress much faster, having become familiar with the snips and the fencing. He continued cutting for just under an hour, and by the time he was done the hole was three-quarters complete.

We took a break then and ate a sandwich apiece and drank a bit of water. We ate without speaking, as we were both busy looking and listening; and by the time we were finished, I had been convinced we were utterly alone at '3 of 3'.

Cutting the rest of the fence was very easy, and before I reached the end, we were able to pull the metal out, fit through with our slings, and pull it back into place. We stood and observed our work: beautiful! From even five feet away one could not tell the fencing had been compromised.

No alarms went off, no lights came on, and no voices ever spoke. The place was shut down prior to the segregations. Those who would handle administration and security were likely in the Elite sector enjoying their week's end with their families. We came at the perfect time.

Without saying a word, we both turned on our heels and proceeded cautiously into the encampment. We were both looking around with our mouths open; the living conditions, while obviously newly constructed, were meager at best, at least from the outside. We made our way to the nearest tent, and as we neared the main door flap, I held my hand out to Barsam to signify that I would go first.

I reached for the flap. It was closed with a common zipping device similar to what we use on our pants or cloaks, but it had a small locking device attached to the control tab. I knelt down and inspected the tiny gadget closely. It was made of much stronger metal than the fences. With that I rooted around in my sling pouch and dug out my multiple-use tool; there was a robust tool with cutting blades on it. It would not have been sufficient for the fence, but it should cut the material of the tent just fine. There was also a serrated saw. It was tiny, but it would help me get through any rough spots I would encounter.

I began to cut, and the job was much more difficult than I anticipated. After only a couple of minutes, I shook my head in disgust. Then I remembered Camira had put a sharp knife in my pouch! I dug it out and turned to see Barsam smiling at me. I rolled my eyes and began cutting once again.

The knife made the job much easier, and while it wasn't going fast, I was able to cut an adequate hole to pass through in the material in about fifteen minutes. I repacked the knife and tool, then poked my head slowly through the opening.

The interior of the tent was dark, very dark. I made a

slight whistle in an attempt to get the attention of anyone who may be inside but received no response. I then dug my small light out and turned it on, and with a deep breath, I shed light directly inside.

I stared around at the stark one-room living space for only a moment before I entered completely, with Barsam on my tail. Once inside I began to get a really good look at the living quarters our loving providers had put together for the people they considered to be the Dregs.

The large single room seemed to be furnished in accordance with differing needs. In one corner was a refrigerated cooler, but from what I could see, there was no freezer on it. There was an automatic speed-cooking unit on a hard metal counter. Above the counter was a single shelf. It held two each of plates, bowls, cups, and saucers. A single pan sink with a faucet, something I had read about only in books, was set in the counter next to the cooking unit. There was a single drawer attached to the counter's underside.

The next corner of the tent was a makeshift toilet and washroom. Once again, there was one small counter with a single-pan sink and faucet. A standing shower cubicle with no door or curtain was in the very corner, and a toilet unit was next to that. Dirt and dust covered everything, and the wet smell of mildew was in the air.

The far right was furnished with two single beds, and each was covered with a rough black blanket and plastic pillow. A small nightstand with a lamp sat between the two beds. I approached and tried the light. The switch clicked hollowly; nothing.

Finally, to the right of the main door flap were two chairs with wooden arms and backs, but the seats were cushioned and covered in a plastic-type material. A table sat before the chairs, void of anything.

"What the hell is this?" Barsam asked, his voice stunned.

I looked around at the filth and bare-bones accommodations once more and said:

"This is '3 of 3'."

CHAPTER 9

Barsam and I made our way quietly around the rest of the camp, entering other tents at random, hoping for improvements in what we saw, but to our dismay, we found all of the tents to be sadly lacking in all possible ways. It didn't bother us in the slightest to damage each and every tent we entered by cutting and hacking at the material. We didn't care that the authorities would discover that the camp had been compromised; as a matter of fact, it made both of us feel very satisfied indeed.

Because of the fact that all the quarters we entered were dismal in the same manner, lacking the basics which provided carefree comfort, we knew it would do no good to enter them all; it would only prove to waste our time. After investigating a handful of them, though, we made our way to the large tent we had seen located at the very rear of the settlement. It would be interesting to see what that tent would be housing.

After cutting our way inside of that particular tent, we knew we had found the 'base of operations' for '3 of 3'. The main entrance area consisted of three desks, with one situated in the center of the room. There were three rows of chairs to the right of the area, situated next to one door flap, and the chairs were obviously for those who would visit the tent for whatever purpose. To the left of the area was another door flap with a sign reading 'Restricted' on the front, and yet another behind the desks. We made our way to it without saying a word to each other.

There was a corridor with a handful of door flaps, both to the left and right of the walkway. Each room we looked into was set up much like a medical facility, with equipment that would be used by doctors during patient visits. We made our way down the hall, and when we got to the end, we encountered yet another door flap, this one wider than all before it. Upon entry, we discovered nothing more than storage for medical supplies.

We returned to the main area, and as we walked, I voiced my observations. "At least those who will be moved here will receive medical attention if they need it."

"Yes," Barsam replied. "I just wonder if it will be

quality care. None of those rooms looked sufficient for long-term medical attention."

We fell into silence once more upon returning to the main area, at which point we crossed the room and approached the door located at the rear of the chairs. The sign on the front of this area read: 'Please Enter the Dining Hall in Single-File Manner Only'. It was a smaller sign, and I had not taken notice of it when we first arrived.

"They will all eat together," Barsam observed aloud.

The communal meals did explain the fact that the other tents had no food preparation appliances. It seemed the new residents of '3 of 3' would enjoy only snacks and small meals in their living quarters. We entered through the flap to find rows of long tables flanked on both sides by plastic chairs. At the farthest point from the door was a serving station where diners would take their plates to be served meals. There was nothing comfortable or homey about the dining area. No wall hangings or plants; it was utterly utilitarian in design.

We didn't spend much time in that area, but made our way back into the entrance room and approached the door located behind the desks. This door had a sign as well. It read simply, 'Storage: Staff Access Only'. This flap had a lock on it, unlike the other two, and I immediately put my knife to the material so we could enter.

Just as the sign said, it appeared to be a storage area only. It seemed to run the entire length of the tent, and it was filled with boxes containing food, blankets, and other essential supplies. At least we knew the residents of '3 of 3' would be kept warm and have their stomachs filled and clothing on their backs if nothing else.

We gave the storage area a good walkthrough, and I concentrated on taking mental notes of all that I observed. We were making our way through the mazes of boxes when I noticed a sign hanging from chains that dangled from the ceiling of the tent. It read, 'Staff Rest Area', and had a red arrow pointing to the rear of the tent.

"Let's check that out, Barsam," I said, and we both headed toward it. Upon arrival at the rear door I pulled my knife out right away; another lock.

The sunlight hit us hard as soon as the flap was open, and I had to squint my eyes against its brightness. Once my eyes adjusted, I saw two tables constructed of wood and a couple of simple garbage bins. The area was surrounded by the same metal fence that surrounded the rest of the compound, but it had a narrow gate set into the middle of it. I had not seen that entrance in the darkness the night before.

"Well," Barsam began, "I guess we have seen everything now."

I walked to the gate. It had no real lock on it, just a simple slide bolt which opened easily enough. I grabbed it and slid the bolt into the open position, and the door swung open effortlessly.

"I want to see past the camp a bit. Farther into the foothills, but not too far. What do you say?"

Barsam looked apprehensive. "Maybe we should be heading back toward home now."

I shook my head. "We cannot stop now. If one of us is segregated, wouldn't you want to know you saw everything? We may miss something important. Besides, where are all the runners from the first segregation?"

Now he looked curious. "Okay, that's a good point. Maybe we can find them. Let's go out, but not too far, Dyzek."

"Fine," I replied. "If we can't find any runners, maybe we can at least find their graves."

We walked through the gate to see what could be found past the settlement.

The sunny day made it easy to see all around us, and we found it much less stressful than the trip in the dark we had made the night before. We talked openly about the new encampment, and neither of us felt good about the situation.

Barsam began. "I will die before I see any of us transferred to this place, Dyzek."

"I feel the same," I replied. "I am glad we came, if for no other reason than to prepare. It is plain now that we must take action if any of us is called away."

I wasn't sure what we would do to avoid segregation if called, but I knew that running and hiding was not going to suffice. Not only would the one hiding be severely punished, but so would the rest for assisting. We would all run and hide together. The only thing left to do was find a safe place to stay.

That was what I was hoping to find by venturing a bit farther into the foothills.

We walked for around an hour, and finally, the foothills began to level off. We were coming out of the thick of the Eloques now. Where did the first runners hide? Could it have been in the very spot where the new camp was located?

"Do you not find it strange that, other than the camp, there is no sign of life out here whatsoever?" I asked Barsam.

"I do," he replied.

No sooner had he answered my question than I saw,

in the distance, a man. He was doing something to the ground, digging or raking, but there was nothing but hard sand, and I could not imagine what he could be doing.

"Dyzek…"

I nodded. "I see him."

Impending Earth

CHAPTER 10

We neared quietly, not wanting to disturb or frighten him. He proved to be much farther away than he appeared, and it took a while to actually reach him. When we were about a quarter span from him, he stood upright to wipe the sweat from his brow; he indeed was digging, and next to him on the ground was a large, dark shape. It lay motionless there.

It was then that the man saw us, and even from our distance, we could see the stricken look of panic that came over his face. He dropped the shovel he had in his hand and turned to run.

"Stop! We mean you no harm!" I yelled. He continued to run, looking over his shoulder in fear. We began to run as well, both of us taking turns yelling as we tried to calm him.

We were gaining on him, and as his level of panic

increased he began to stumble, finally tripping over his own feet and falling to the ground in a heap. We passed the spot where he had been digging, and I tried to identify the bundle lying on the ground, but to no avail. It didn't matter as much as speaking to the stranger did.

We gained on him quickly. He was struggling to rise to his feet when we finally reached him, and when we put our hands on him to help him up, he began to scream for help.

"We are not going to hurt you!" I spoke severely to him in an effort to get and keep his attention. "We only want to talk to you, man!"

His eyes were filled with fear and panic, so I lowered my voice and continued to reassure him. We kept a tight grip on his torn, dirty cloak so he could not run again. After a few moments of constant reassurance, he began to calm down, and he finally collapsed to the ground, sobbing.

I immediately sat down next to him in the red dirt. "I am Dyzek," I began. "This is Barsam. What is your name?"

He looked up at me with yellowing blue eyes, tears running down his face. "Al— Aldan. My name is Aldan."

The strength seemed to have drained from his body, and finally, his tears subsided. "We do not want to harm you, as I have said. We only wanted to see the new compound. Why are you here?"

Aldan took a ragged breath. "I have been here since the segregation. My wife died, and I only wanted to bury her properly."

I looked at Barsam, but he took no notice. He continued to look at the man with great compassion in his eyes. "I am sorry you have lost your wife, sir," he said.

The man tried to stand then, and we helped him the rest of his way to his feet. He was dirty and smelly as if he hadn't bathed in some time. Even the hair on his head and his beard were matted with dirt. He was probably in his sixth decade, I guessed, though he looked to be a bit older. He was virtually skin and bones, and his flesh bore the yellow hue of feeble health.

Now Aldan began to make his way back toward his shovel, and the bundle that was his wife's body. "We will help you, sir, if you wish," I said to him.

Aldan turned to me slightly as he walked. "Yes," he replied. "I could use the help."

We reached the spot, I picked up the shovel and began to dig. The smell of his deceased wife was a bit overwhelming, and I had to stop to tie my head covering over my face in order to bear it; Barsam did the same, but

Aldan didn't seem to be bothered by the smell at all. He sat on the ground and watched, his hands trembling and tears running freely from his eyes as he did so.

"There was no one to help when she became sick," he said simply, out of the blue.

I stopped and gave him my attention, but he did not continue. I gave Barsam a look, and he reached out for the shovel to take a turn digging. I sat on the ground next to Aldan then, in silence. Finally, he spoke again.

"Why have they put up the tents?" he asked.

I looked at him carefully. "They are going to segregate once again."

Aldan began to laugh, and a crazy sound it was. "I am not surprised," he finally said. "They will continue until only those they have chosen are left."

"We thought they were happy after the initial segregation," I told him. "It seems they feel the need to do it again, though."

"Ha!" Aldan said sharply. "Do you not understand what is truly happening?"

I shook my head, confused. Barsam stopped digging and looked at us both, listening intently. He looked as confused as I felt.

Now that Aldan had our full attention he decided to talk, really talk. "I worked for the main government, in an excellent position. I wrote announcements for the priest, preparing them for the daily broadcasts."

"You were one of the Elite?" I asked.

Aldan nodded. "Yes, but in the end, I knew too much."

Barsam spoke. "What do you mean, 'too much'?" he asked.

"I found out about the quasar," he stated simply.

I shook my head, more confused than ever. "What quasar?"

Aldan turned his eyes to the sky, which he scanned with a faraway look. "Only a couple of months before the segregation, the first one, the quasar was discovered. The Washans brought it to the attention of our government, and it was then confirmed to exist."

"Aldan," I began, my voice a bit sharp in my frustration. "You are making no sense. What quasar?"

After only a moment he met my eyes, then looked at Barsam as well before continuing. "The Washans came to our heads of state and made them aware that a quasar, a jet of high-frequency radiation which is, utterly destructive to anything it comes into contact with, is heading toward Marmara on a direct collision course.

"At first no one believed them, as the quasar was, at

that point, undetectable with any of the instruments we have. The Washans persisted, adamant that our planet was doomed, and all they wanted to do was help." Aldan cleared his throat then ran his hands through his ragged head of hair. "After many, many meetings, which the Washans called in an effort to 'save' our peoples, our government became convinced, at least enough to pay attention to the instruments the Washans had on their home planet. One of which was a portable gazing unit which they had brought with them during their teleportation to our planet."

"Why has this quasar not hit us, if it exists?" Barsam asked.

Aldan turned to him. "Why, it is still in route. It travels very, very fast, but it is extremely far; nonetheless, it's any moment in the next few months in which contact will occur."

He looked down at his dirt-covered hands and continued. "So, the priest and all of his so-called 'advisors' decided to take a look at the supposed threat, which they did, using the Washans' gazing device, and sure enough, it was hurtling through the stars right for us.

The segregations are nothing more than our government's way of singling out the most healthy, beautiful, and pure for salvation." Now he looked me directly in the eyes as if to measure my reaction.

I processed what Aldan had told us, but only for a moment. "So, what you are telling us is that, as we speak, a quasar is coming, and it will annihilate this planet at some point in the future?"

"The near future," he replied. "And sooner than I thought if they are conducting a second segregation. You see, it already destroyed the faraway planet of Washa. Why do you really think they came? To save themselves, and when it was discovered that we, too, are in its path, they decided to convince our government to enact the segregations."

"So that only the best and most brilliant will survive," Barsam said.

Aldan nodded. "Exactly."

"What happened? Why are you hiding?" I questioned, doubting the story Aldan told us. "If you worked under the priest you are an Elite. What you are saying makes no sense! The first segregation is long over, and nothing has happened. All of this isolation has gone to your head and driven you mad!"

Aldan shook his head and held my eyes. "It is extremely powerful with energy. From here one can see it at night, but it looks just like another one of the stars.

No, Dyzek, my newfound friend. It is coming."

We all fell into silence, and my mind was racing faster than I could keep up. Impending disaster did explain why our government would separate us, but did the Elite already know? I highly doubted it. There had not been a hint of panic from anyone. So who did know? Only the government and the most trusted members of it?

"When the Washans were first able to prove the quasar's existence to us, it was up to me to prepare a speech for the priest for announcements, but before it was even complete it was canceled, per the Washan's advice," Aldan continued. "They convinced the government that mass chaos would ensue, should the people find out about the pending disaster, and they reassured us that it would take much time to make the proper preparations.

"The more I thought about it, the more I knew I could not keep the news to myself, and I approached the priest to let him know that it was wrong to keep the people in the dark," he said. "Things had been going so well and had been so peaceful on Marmara. Our government had no way to control or contain the panic that would occur."

Barsam interjected. "So the Washans shared their original plan, the plan for the best to survive."

"Yes!" Aldan's eyes lit up with excitement as he

realized that we were beginning to get it, beginning to believe. "They have yet another planet, an unknown distant planet, chosen already for all of the Elite, both Washan and Marmaran alike, to relocate to and live on. They will simply teleport before zero hour."

"Leaving the Mids, and now the Dregs, here to die," I spat with disgust.

Aldan smiled bitterly. "It is a small price to pay. There is no way all can be transported; even at the rate the quasar is moving, it would literally take decades to relocate everyone. Only one can transport at a time, you see."

He cleared his throat and looked at the sky once again. "So, they were going to initially keep me and segregate my dear wife, the gods rest her soul. Once they realized I would not keep quiet and cooperate, they were going to do me in. How I do not know. What I do know is that I didn't wait around to find out.

"I was going to die no matter what, and I knew it, so I decided to take a risk on living, and I ran with my wife," he said, his eyes tearing up. "Who knew? Maybe the quasar would miss us, and we would live our lives on Marmara with the rest of the runners."

My head snapped up as he caught my attention.

"There are others? Where are they?"

"There were others," Aldan replied. "They lived at the very spot where the new camp is now. They were all executed before the camp was set up, and piled up and burned on the other side of the Eloques. Only my wife Dahria and I escaped, and they never came looking."

Barsam turned to me then, his eyes filled with fear. "Dyzek, if this is true, what are we to do?"

I fell silent. There was so much to ponder and sort out, and I was in no way ready to even begin doing this. Both Aldan and Barsam watched my face for any reaction.

Finally, I spoke. "Right now we will finish burying Aldan's wife. Aldan, if it is okay with you, we will stay until nightfall; I would like to see what I can of this quasar. Then we will return home. The second segregations begin in only two days, and we need to be there when they begin. Let's hope that none of us are included, at least not right away."

"Do you have wives?" Aldan asked.

Barsam smiled. "Yes, we do. Their names are Morgayne and Camira. They wait for us to return home with news on what we have found here."

"They are afraid?"

"Aldan," I replied, "we are all afraid."

We spent the remainder of that day with our new friend, the runner Aldan. He brought us to the place he called home since the first segregation, a cave he had dug out of the side of a foothill with his own bare hands. The entrance was away from the encampment so it wouldn't be easily seen, and he had hidden the entrance with a makeshift door made of dirt and shrubs.

We ate with him, a meal of toasted salamander and makoko tree leaves. It was not delicious, by any means, but it was filling, and we left him with our last two sandwiches, which pleased him greatly. As night fell we positioned ourselves outside the door of his cave to see the approaching doom that awaited us.

"When I first ran, one could not see the quasar with the naked eye," Aldan began as we settled on the ground. "Now I can easily see it with the aid of this." He produced a long, narrow-looking glass, the kind one might use to observe their enemies from afar in battle. "It grows a bit bigger in my lens every night that passes."

It was still a bit light out when we sat, but it quickly grew much darker. I looked into the sky in silence. All of the stars could be clearly seen, and while some twinkled a bit brighter than others, they all looked the same to me. I waited patiently for Aldan, who was already looking through the lens, to share and show us this quasar, but Barsam could barely contain himself. He was nearly hopping.

After nearly half an hour, Aldan steered the lens to me. Before I put it up to my eye, he pointed at one particularly bright star. "It is there, the brightest one near the Contabula constellation."

I knew Contabula well from my days of education and found it easily enough with my naked eye. I then located the star he pointed to and put the lens to my eye so I could get a better look. I did not expect what I saw.

Through the lens, it continued to look like nothing more than a simple star, but as I focused on the target I realized: it was moving. Yes, it was barely noticeable, but it was moving, nonetheless, and it was heading in this direction.

Aldan spoke. "With the equipment, the Washans have you would be able to see it much, much better. Do you see? Do you see it coming for us?"

"I see," I replied quietly. All I could really do was stare, and I knew in my soul that everything Aldan had told us was true.

Barsam began to lose control of himself. "Dyzek! Let me look!"

I handed him the lens, but my eyes remained fastened

on the star lookalike that was flying toward us at what was likely a breakneck pace in reality. "I wonder how long we have," I thought aloud.

"Well," Aldan replied, "If they are segregating once again, I would guess no more than two months. Perhaps three, but I would not count on three."

Barsam's breathing was heavy as he focused. I was still looking at the bright quasar, watching it twinkle as it moved and wondering how something so violent could appear so beautiful. It didn't matter, I knew. The best thing I could do at this point was to come up with a way to spend my last living days with those I loved.

Or formulate an accurate plan of escape.

Finally, I spoke. "Barsam, we need to get back home. It is time now."

He did not respond to me right away, and I had to take him by the shoulder and shake him a bit to get his attention. After a moment he handed the lens back to Aldan, his eyes fixed on the quasar in the sky. "It is coming for us, Dyzek," he said in a low, distant voice.

"Yes," I replied, resigned to the fact. "It is coming."

I stood up then, with Barsam and Aldan right behind me. I reached for Aldan's hand to shake it, but he grasped me in a firm hug. Afterward, he embraced Barsam as well, then he stepped back and looked at us both.

"Whatever you do, be careful. Perhaps it is better for two or three of you to survive in the new world than for all of you to perish."

I shook my head vigorously. "I understand your way of thinking, Aldan, but I will die before I live at the cost of the lives of any of my loved ones."

"Me as well," Barsam agreed.

Aldan nodded and reached out, patting me on the shoulder. "I understand. Just as I would not be separated from my beloved, you will not be separated from those you love."

"Aldan, if we come up with a plan, if we formulate a way to escape the destruction, do you want to come with us?" I knew that, no matter what, only the Elite would live if I did not act; the four of us were Mids. We would not survive no matter what. I needed to come up with something, and I needed to do it fast.

"If you find a way, and it is within your power to fetch me, I will go," Aldan replied. "But keep in mind that death for me is nothing more than unification with my wife, and with that I am content."

With that, the three of us parted ways, Aldan into his safe haven, and Barsam and I back toward the encampment and home. We would not enter the camp again; rather, we would go around the foothill that flanked its rear. Both of us were ready to get home to the women, and my mind was working furiously on the disastrous problem that lay before us.

We had walked for only about an hour when I realized that I was no longer concerned about supervisors or other authority figures discovering us. "Barsam, what do you think about all we have learned?" I asked my companion out loud.

He cleared his throat. "I think we must find a solution or die trying."

"Yes," I responded. "It is as simple as that, isn't it?"

"It is."

We continued to walk, and after a moment I said the obvious. "There is only one way, Barsam."

"I am glad you know," he said. "As far as I am concerned, we are as good as dead. I can think of nothing."

"No. There is one way and one way only," I continued. "We must find the Washan's transporter, and we must leave Marmara. We must leave all of them behind, and see to it they can never follow, or all of this will only happen again and again."

I had no idea how to carry out such a plan. I knew

with a bath, a hot meal, and good sleep I would think more clearly. We both focused our attention on the journey home. When I had my wits about me, I would do my planning.

The second segregations would begin the evening after next.

CHAPTER 11

We arrived at the rear of our home in the dark hours of the next morning, with the stars still twinkling, though fading, as the sun rose to the west. Both of the girls would be asleep, as it was still the task week's end. I could hardly wait to eat, clean up, and snuggle next to Camira's warm body. I was utterly exhausted, both mentally and physically.

We entered quietly through the main door, with the use of my key card. We then placed our sling bags gently on the floor and made our way into the food preparation room to eat, and we did all of this in silence. I did not want to wake the women and be confronted with hordes of questions; it would be enough to talk about everything after we were rested up.

We ate hot meat sandwiches and soup with vegetables, and then I told Barsam to get cleaned up first.

I would clean up our food preparation mess, and it would give me some time alone to think. He stole off for the bathing room without argument.

As I slid the dishes into the cleansing unit, I thought about the transporter unit the Washans had used to come to Marmara. It would be the only means of escape from the destruction traveling our way. I had no idea where it could be kept, but I knew that it was likely located in the main government offices, in the Elite section. I worked there, but there were so many buildings and sections to each that I had no idea where to begin my search.

All I could do was put one foot in front of the other, and hope for our salvation. Segregation or not, we would die if we did not find a way off Marmara, and I would not let that happen while lying down. But what was the proper first step to take?

I often ran office errands while on task, and many times these errands required that I travel to other sections and buildings. I was aware of which buildings the Washans used, and I was sure the transport would be located in one of those. The problem was that one was hardly ever sent on errands to one of the Washan buildings. It was not unheard-of, but it was very infrequent.

I had run errands to run there a couple of times, but

I could probably count them on one hand. They were always to deliver messages only. Perhaps I could steal away at night and break into the main building of the Washan's governmental quarters? My head was swimming. I needed to stop obsessing. Tomorrow would bring me a new perspective.

The sun was on full rise by the time I had a shower and crawled in bed next to Camira. I thought about waking her to make love, but even as I pondered the thought, I fell into a deep sleep. The rest of our lives were before us, no matter how short, to indulge in that, I supposed.

∞

"Dyzek? Dyzek, wake up!" It was Camira's soft voice, rousing me from my deep rest. "Why didn't you wake me when you got home?"

I turned to her, realizing she was shaking my shoulder. "I didn't want to. You were sleeping so soundly."

"Well?" she asked, her eyes wide with both apprehension and excitement. "What did you find?"

I sat up and ran my fingers through my hair, then rubbed my eyes. "Camira, you have to give me a bit to wake all the way up. What time is it?"

"About an hour and a half until lunch. You should get moving. I will bring you a morning beverage to get you going," she replied, and with that, she stood, still in her sleeping clothes, and left the room quickly.

I put my feet on the floor and my head in my hands, trying to rub my head and eyes awake. Evidently, I would have slept all day, had she not woken me. It was time to get around, though, as I had to fill in the girls and begin to consider our next move.

For a brief moment it seemed as if our trip to '3 of 3' was nothing more than a dream, as was Aldan and the quasar, but as reality set in, I knew nothing could be further from the truth. Yes, there were tents in a new encampment, set up for the 'Dregs'. Yes, there was an older man living alone in the foothills whose wife Barsam and I helped bury, and, yes, a quasar was going to crash into Marmara and kill every living thing. Another hour of sleep was an hour wasted that should be spent thinking and planning.

I was just pulling my shirt over my head when Camira appeared bearing a huge steaming mug of coffee, black, just the way I liked it. "Good morning," I said to her timidly.

"Good morning," she replied softly. "I would raise my voice at you for not waking me when you came in, but you seemed to be so content and sleeping so soundly…"

I responded in a tone conducive to her comfort. "I was exhausted. These few hours of sleep have given me great rest."

I continued to dress without speaking, and Camira sat on the edge of the unmade bed and watched me in silence. Finally, she spoke. "Are you ready to talk about the journey?"

I looked at Camira and smiled flirtatiously out of the corner of my mouth. "I would love to. I just need a bit of breakfast and coffee first, if that is okay?"

Camira held out her hand to me, and I took it. It was the first feeling of satisfaction I'd had in days, and it pleased me greatly to do so. I wrapped my fingers around hers, which were warm and soft beyond measure, and I allowed myself to feel the comfort and contentment they provided.

"I do have a lot to tell you, and not all of it will you consider 'good'." My words were not meant for preparation as much as a confirmation. Confirmation that I was there for her and the rest of my family. Confirmation that I was here, and I was willing.

My days with Camira had been plentiful, I could say,

even if they were to end tomorrow. I had read many stories of love and faithfulness between the two sexes, but I never looked at my relationship with her as one...until now. Now I saw it for what it was: to see each other through to the end or die trying, for both of us. The world we lived in tried to make love between a man and a woman something it could never be. Something perfect and very far out of reach. My relationship with Camira would forever be just out of reach, but always within my grasp, and I knew this full well.

At that moment I would always be with her, and I knew it.

I took her hand and allowed my love to pull me to my feet. I had information, and she had common sense and strength. Together we would come to grips with the knowledge I had gained and exercise our power in regard to what to do with that information.

The future was up to us entirely.

∞

I took my seat at the table in our home, the one where we took our meals in the main dining area. Camira set another fresh cup of dark black coffee before me, and I wrapped my fingers around the curved handle. The vessel felt warm and comforting, I tore my attention away from it and focused my eyes on the two women and the man who sat with me: my family; my lover and my best friends.

We all sat quietly for several minutes and took our beverage, Barsam and I clearing the sleep from our heads. Finally, when the girls could take no more of the silence, Camira broke it gently.

"So, I guess we are more than ready to hear about Eloques," she stated plainly.

I looked at Barsam, who stared into his cup, then I looked at each of the girls. "We found the new sector easily enough."

"And?"

"And it is bare bones," I replied. "Those to be segregated there will not be happy with the living conditions. It is nothing more than tents with the most basic of necessities. It is not at all anything like what we have been provided with here, and far less than the Elite are enjoying."

I took a long draw from my beverage, then stood to refill it. Camira jumped up and grabbed my cup, so I sat back down. "The new encampment is truly the least of our worries, girls."

Now Morgayne's eyes grew wide and filled with

confusion. "What do you mean, Barsam?"

"Give me just a bit longer," I said. "I need to clear my head better to discuss it properly."

"We'll get some food for the two of you." Camira touched Morgayne's arm, and the girls went into the main food preparation room to prepare a couple of plates with whatever breakfast fare our wonderful government had provided for the Mids that day.

I looked back at Barsam, who was giving me his full attention now. "What are you going to tell them?" he asked, his eyes shifting back and forth between the girls and me.

"The truth, of course. How can we work together and have a chance at successfully surviving if I lie to them the way we have been lied to?"

Our food came in minutes, and we ate in silence. After the plates were cleared and our cups filled again the girls sat down and looked at me expectantly. There was no avoiding it, and I didn't want to.

"Okay, ladies, here it is," I began. "After we investigated the new sector, which was nothing more than a camp, really, we ventured past the foothills a bit further. I was hoping to find runners or at least a place we could hide if one or more of us were on the segregation list."

"What did you find?" Camira asked.

I took another drink as Barsam tinkered nervously with his cup. "First, I want you both to keep calm, no matter what I say. Second, I want everything said here to stay here. No gossiping about it at the task sites, understand?"

Both girls nodded vigorously, and I continued. "We encountered an older man by the name of Aldan. I didn't know him or remember him from before the first segregations, but he had lived there since then. He was burying his wife when we first saw him."

"Oh, how sad!" Morgayne's hand flew to her mouth, and her eyes welled up with compassionate tears, but she continued to give me her full attention.

"He had actually been a direct employee of the government, writing announcement materials for the priest himself," I said. "He would have actually been classified as an Elite, if not for the circumstances."

Camira maintained sharp eye contact with me, not allowing me to look away, her eyes narrow and serious. "What circumstances?"

"I am going to start from what I understand to be the beginning. Please don't ask too many questions, because I simply don't have any answers yet," I said, then drained my cup and set it down.

"The Washans did not come to Marmara as simple explorers who wanted to share their great knowledge," I began. "They came here because they knew Marmara could sustain life, and they were facing mass destruction."

Barsam rose, taking both of our cups for a final refill. I continued. "Their planet, which was quite far from this one, was in the direct path of a quasar, and they had to relocate to survive."

Camira looked a bit confused. "A quasar?"

"A quasar is an object in space, conjured from energy, and is very bright," I said. "I really can't explain the science of it, but it looks like a star to the eye. It is very destructive. It has already destroyed Washa."

"What does this have to do with us?" Morgayne asked.

I met her gaze. "The Washans arrived to find Marmara inhabited, at least that is what I assume. They also discovered that Marmara was also in the quasar's path. It will take time, but the quasar is going to hit Marmara as well."

Both girls sucked in their breath sharply, almost in unison. Camira spoke, her voice filled with anxiety and tension. "We are all going to die? This doesn't make sense! Why the segregations?"

"I am getting to that, love!" My voice was sharper than I wanted it to be. "I am sorry. Please ask questions when I am done, or I will continue to lose my thoughts."

After I regathered my thoughts, I continued. "Now, escape from the planet can be done only by teleportation, which the Washans have. Since their arrival here, there has not been enough time to teleport everyone to the new safe planet, which Aldan said they have already chosen." I stopped just long enough to take a drink from my cup, and Barsam continued for me.

"Even if we began the teleportation process the second they arrived, the machine can supposedly only transfer one person at a time. The quasar would have destroyed the remaining people on the planet before the process was complete," Barsam said.

I picked up the ball again. "Not only that, but the Washans are willing to have only the 'purest' of our people transfer with them. They desire a totally Elite society, with no drainage on the people whatsoever."

Barsam said, "So they began to convince our government to segregate, just once in the beginning, and now once again, so as to distract us, I would guess."

A look of disgust filled Camira's face. "So, they would get us off, alone and helpless, without each other's assistance, and they would leave us behind to be destroyed."

"They are murdering us," Morgayne finished.

"Yes," I said simply. "And they will survive."

We sat quietly and allowed this necessary information to sink into the girls' minds. Finally, I said, "I think I am ready to answer whatever questions I can answer."

Camira stated, "I wonder what it looks like, this 'quasar'."

"Just like a star," I replied. "Aldan had a looking glass and showed it to us. It looks like a star that is getting closer and closer all the time."

Barsam then said, "That is why Aldan took to the hills. He refused to keep this classified information to himself. He wanted to let all the peoples know the truth, and they threatened to take his life and segregate his wife. Aldan refused to be separated from his wife, so they ran."

"The rest of those who ran are dead," I added. "killed by the government for running, and their bodies are piled up further east on the other side of the Eloques; we did not see them. Aldan told us. He and his wife were not captured, and she recently passed from illness."

"How long until the quasar hits?" Morgayne asked.

Barsam gave her the answer, his voice low and gentle. "Between two and three months, Aldan estimates."

The girls held their emotions in check very well, though Camira reached across the table to hold Morgayne's trembling hand. Finally, Morgayne spoke, "Being separated is the very least of our worries, my friends."

"Indeed," I replied.

Morgayne replied in a determined voice. "What are our options?"

I sat back in my chair and cleared my throat. "I have been thinking, and we really have only one, if we want to live, that is." I fell into silence.

"Well?" Camira asked. "What is it?"

I looked at her and smiled a grim smile, one that did not touch my eyes. "We must locate the teleportation machine and basically steal it, but we must stop anyone from following us, or we will be as good as dead anyway."

Morgayne stood up, her eyes crazy and flashing. "That is your plan? We don't even have an idea as to where it would be, much less how it works if we found it! And how would we even begin to know how to stop them from following us?" Her voice was high, and she was beginning to panic.

"Morgayne, we need to remain calm," I began. She sat down, her breathing rapid and haggard. Camira moved her chair around the table and embraced the girl, who buried her head in Camira's shoulder.

I gave Camira a bittersweet smile and continued. "I don't think it is at all impossible. Consider: the device is going to be located somewhere in the area where the Washans live and conduct business. Our government is going to know the location. It can be found."

I stood and began to walk around the room, thinking as I spoke. "Just as we know the device is here, we know that operational instructions exist. I work in the classified information section. At this point, I will go to whatever lengths I need to in order to find both."

Barsam chimed in. "Once we discover those things, we must figure out a way to destroy the traces of us evacuating."

"However, when we destroy it," I replied, "I will be that last person. I will see to it that no one follows."

I thought for only a moment. "If any of us are announced when the new segregations begin, that person will be hidden. We will take them, that very night, to Aldan. He will keep them until our plan is solid and ready to be carried out. I want him to join us anyway."

"How do you intend to find this teleporter?" Camira asked. "What is in your mind, Dyzek?"

"Well," I began, "I see it this way: at this point, none

of us have anything to lose except each other. Even if we are not included in these new segregations, we are going to be left behind for destruction, as we are not included in the Elite."

I continued. "Beginning the first day of the task week, I will take any extra errands into the main government buildings if any are offered. Even if they are not, I will take my midday meal breaks to explore and search."

"You are taking great risks, Dyzek," Morgayne stated, breaking her silence.

I nodded solemnly. "If we stay, we die. If I am caught, we die. To stand still and do nothing is to take the greatest risk of all."

I went on. "All of us should be keeping our eyes and ears open at all times. On the first day of the week, I am going to do a bit of 'breaking' into the system, but I am going to use a co-worker's passcode, someone who will not cause any suspicion. I know that the location of the teleport device, as well as instructions for use, are going to be in there somewhere."

"Whose passcode will you use?" Barsam asked.

I looked at the ground, feeling a bit of shame. "My own cousin, Maron's."

Now Camira's eyes grew wide with disbelief. "Dyzek!

He has been helpful to us in the past! How could you do that?"

"How could I not?" I was beginning to feel much frustration and anger. "Do you think if he could willingly help us he would? And do you think he would give up his Elite position and salvation and trade it for yours? Or Morgayne's? No! He would not, he will not, and he will teleport to the new planet willingly, smiling with content that his own life has been spared!"

I continued. "Make no mistake: the little help Maron has given us is out of guilt for the reality of the situation here on Marmara, but when it comes to sparing his own life he will feel none."

"You will certainly be caught by him, and he will tell," Morgayne said quietly.

"Yes," I replied. "But make no mistake, I will take his life for the sake of saving all of yours. I will do what I must!"

Camira opened her mouth as if to say something, but I gave her a look that told her to keep quiet. Nothing she could do would change my mind. What had to be done, had to be done. No one on Marmara who was an Elite, which was everyone but them at this point, would care what happened to us. I would rather die in a full-blown rebellion, attempting to begin a new life and live it, than if I were huddled in a frightened ball, waiting for our DNA to be deconstructed upon intense radiation.

"Now, on the first day of the task week, I will begin my search," I said with a solid voice, filled with determination. "None of you need to do anything but watch and listen, and let me know if you learn anything of magnitude. Otherwise, just be ready to do as I instruct when the time comes. I will fill you all in each night. It is as simple as that."

"And as for the week's end, on those days I will be acting in accordance with what I have learned during the week."

Barsam spoke. "Whatever you do, wherever you go, I will follow, brother."

"And I," said Camira.

Morgayne met my eyes. "And I as well."

I took a deep breath and let it out with a resigned sigh. "So it shall be. Now let us enjoy our day. I am going to use it to go through some of the manuals I have put away from my task. I may be able to find something in the map sections that may give away the location of the teleport device, though I have no idea what." I thought for only a moment. "Try to put this out of your mind and let Barsam and me handle it. Trust us as your lovers and caregivers, please."

The women nodded and made their way out of the dining area. Camira turned around right before she was out of the room and said, "I am going to have Morgayne help me out in the flower garden. We will be there if either of you needs us, and we will see you at the midday meal." With that, she turned and left.

Barsam said, "So, you think the manual's maps may hold some information?"

"Well," I replied, "they were issued directly after the first segregation for all employees. Whether ours are the same as the Elite's I, do not know, but there may be something that points us in the right direction." I went to the closet in the entryway of our home, and from it, I pulled out a set of four books, each about three inches thick.

I took Manual 1 and handed Manual 2 to Barsam. "The maps are in the last two chapters of each, and the maps apply only to major buildings in the Elite section. We need to look each one over thoroughly. Look for any rooms in any sections that don't have a clear explanation of their use is."

Barsam nodded and opened his book right away. I grabbed a notebook of paper and a couple of writing utensils, then sat down, to begin with my own manual.

When I opened it I recognized the small print of the maps immediately, though I had never given them any real attention. There was quite a bit of information, and all of it seemed very detailed.

I looked up at Barsam. "It is going to be a long day, brother."

Impending Earth

CHAPTER 12

By the midday meal, Barsam and I were finished with the maps in the first two manuals. On a single page in the notebook, I had made notes on only three areas found in those manuals. None of the three were marked with information regarding what they were used for, or even marked 'Closed'. They were simply blank areas of supposed 'wasted space'; which is likely how the government is hiding this teleporter.

Two of them were located near the living and working areas of the Washans, but I didn't want to get my hopes up, for we still had two more manuals to go over. By the time we wrapped up the first two our midday meals had long gone cold, and Camira and Morgayne re-heated our food just to make it palatable.

"I feel good about what we have found," Barsam said as he scooped vegetables into his mouth with a spoon.

"While I know we are still in the dark, just the fact that we have found something is like a light at the end of a long, dark tunnel."

"I agree." I took a bite of my meat and made a face; it wasn't good at all after being reheated and tasted a bit like I would imagine building board to taste. Barsam chuckled at me as I moved it aside and turned to my own vegetables. "Very funny. Anyway, it seems that there should be some type of marking. I don't think they ever expected anyone to give the maps in the manuals any mind. I think they thought everyone other than the Elites are too stupid to even think that way."

Barsam nodded. "That would be their mistake, then, wouldn't it?"

I was anxious to get to the next manuals, and gobbled the rest of my food, leaving the meat for the garbage disposal unit. We both washed our meal down with cold milk and then rose from the table to resume our project, leaving the plates for the girls to clean up.

The rest of the afternoon was just like the morning. We scanned the maps in the last two manuals thoroughly and then gave all four manuals one last going over for good measure. By the time we were finished, we still only had one page of notes featuring a total of five areas that were either not marked or not marked clearly. All five of them were either within Washan living space or in very close proximity to it. To me, that information spoke volumes.

We closed the books once and for all, and I looked at Barsam. "I have a good feeling about the work we have done. While there are five areas to investigate, at least we have an idea. The teleportation device has to be in one of them."

"Absolutely," Barsam replied, his eyes alight. "It could be in no other, as we are basically familiar with all other areas and their uses, wouldn't you agree?"

"Yes," I said. "I am going to begin at the beginning of the work week. My course of action will involve getting away from my task station and investigating them one at a time."

"You will need some kind of weapon or protection, Dyzek."

I nodded. Barsam was right; I couldn't simply venture into areas the government had made 'off limits' to us Mids. That would be outright defiance of the laws and our new ways. If I were discovered by someone who recognized me as a Mid, I would likely have to defend myself, but what could I use?

The only weapon type anyone on Marmara had, other

than patrolling supervisors and other authoritative people, were knives. Other weapons were outlawed and confiscated before the first segregations. It would have to do.

"I will take two knives," I told Barsam. "One for each hand. That way I will be dually protected, in the case that one is knocked away."

He shook his head at me. "I think you should take a couple of spares. Keep them inside of your foot-liners inside of your shoes, or maybe in your cloak pockets. You can never be too safe, Dyzek."

"You are right. I will take four." I looked over my notes. "Okay, let's take the map pages out of the manuals that correspond with the unmarked sections. We should have done that before, but I wasn't thinking."

"No worries," Barsam stated. "At least we wrote down enough to be able to turn right to them."

It only took us twenty minutes or so to find the map pages and tear them out of the manuals. I made sure each page had enough information for me to find the desired location. If it did not, I removed the other pages that went with it to help me along. I had a feeling that, not only were we going to locate the teleport device, but we were going to live through the terrible nightmare that Marmara had become during our lifetimes.

∞

Dinner was hot chicken and mashed potato root. It was piping hot this time, and extraordinarily delicious. I looked forward to the meal for more than the food. I was anxious to relate to the girls all that we had found.

As soon as we sat, Barsam and I tore into our plates; we were both quite ravenous after having only milk and vegetables for our lunch. The women were patient, waiting for us both to eat, but they barely touched their own food. Finally, after a few heaping bites I looked up at their expectant faces.

"Well, I believe I have good news all the way around," I began. "Barsam and I were able to find five locations that were unspecified on all of Marmara, and all five of them are located near Washan living and working space."

Camira smiled, her eyes lighting up, and Morgayne let out an audible sigh of relief. "That's good!" Camira said. "I am so relieved. To be honest, I expected you to find nothing!"

Barsam spoke up. "Yes. We already figured that our government did not expect anyone to ever look or take notice."

"They have taken us all for morons," Morgayne said simply.

I nodded, a smile covering my face. "Indeed."

We continued to eat. The evening announcements would begin after supper, but the segregation announcements would not start until tomorrow. While it made me nervous to know they were nearly upon us, I was also feeling much freer. Even if they did announce one or more of us, we would be able to deal with it. Aldan was our safety net; we would all come out of this fine, I just knew it.

"My next course of action is to arm myself and begin to investigate the unmarked sections one at a time," I stated. "I intend to take knives, four of them in all. I will have two in my hands, hidden beneath the sleeves of my cloak, and I will have two more backup knives in the rear pockets of my trousers, so they are easily accessible in case one or more are knocked from my hands."

Camira thought for a moment. "You may not be recognized as a Mid at all, depending on who you encounter."

We finished our meal and cleaned up quickly before making our way into the main area and turning on the large screen. Pleasant music and a scene with animals and flowers were on it, passing the time for viewers until the announcements began. The scenes were meant to be conducive to peace and tranquility, and they had been a part of the life of all Mids since the first segregations. Now I merely saw them as another underhanded method of mind control, and it made me angry and sick to my stomach.

Finally, the announcements began. "Good evening, Marmara. It looks to be a wonderful new week, and we are pleased to announce the completion of the beautiful new accommodations at '3 of 3'. We are very excited to provide for those of you who will be residing there. Keep in mind that residents to be transferred will be announced on the first, third, and fifth days of each work week until complete.

We look forward to making you all content and comfortable!"

"Pathetic liars," Barsam grumbled under his breath.

Announcements continued, first telling us what our weather would be like tomorrow, and then going on to the tasks. As if nothing were amiss, all of our tasks would carry on, as usual, meaning Barsam and Morgayne would work their night shifts that night. When announcements were complete, they both stood.

"I suppose we had better get some kind of sleep," Morgayne said, stretching out as she stood. "Even if it only is a few short hours." They retired together, leaving

Camira and me alone for the first time to talk.

She reached for my hand and took it in her own, so I turned to face her. "I can't tell you how relieved I am that you found something, anything, in the manuals, Dyzek."

"I know," I replied. "I really thought everything would be marked, even in a misleading manner, and I was prepared to have to do some kind of 'code-breaking', so to speak."

I gave her hand a squeeze and continued. "It appears our government believes the very worst about anyone that they do not consider 'Elite'. They seem to believe we cannot even think for ourselves."

"It is good that they think that way," Camira replied. "It gives us the upper hand in the end."

I looked into her beautiful brown eyes. No matter how all of this came out, no matter what happened in the end, my love for her would never die, even if I did. I suddenly felt compelled to kiss her, and I held nothing back. I leaned forward and, taking her by the back of the head, pressed my lips against hers with great urgency. She responded with passion, her tongue finding its way to mine, her hands tangling in my blond hair.

We continued kissing, and after a moment she began to press her body against mine. My hands began to roam freely, and as I kissed her, I enjoyed the feel of her breasts, her hips, and the warmth between her legs. Our breathing became very heavy, and our hands were out of control.

She pulled away from me, gasping for breath. "We should go into our room, Dyzek," she panted in a whisper. "One of them could come out at any time." She was smiling shyly, and I realized how over-ready I was to feel her nakedness in full.

She stood and took my hand, pulling me to my feet. She didn't have to convince me; I leaped up willingly and with great eagerness. I stopped her as she started to pull me to the bedroom. She turned to me, with a questioning look in her eyes. "What is it?"

My smile faded as I looked at her face, with its perfect curves and deep color. Her high cheekbones were so striking! While I knew of them and had admired them countless times, they seemed more prominent to me than ever before, and her almond-shaped brown eyes were so bottomless I thought I would get lost in them then and there.

"You are truly the most beautiful woman I have ever seen, my Camira," I whispered, my voice hoarse. The thought of losing her made me want to weep.

She stopped and came to me, pulling me into a warm

embrace. "I love you, Dyzek. I always have, and I will until the end of time."

I closed my eyes, and my lips sought hers blindly, I found and kissed them madly. Somehow we made our way into our room and fell onto our warm bed in a tangled heap. Our hands were everywhere, touching and feeling each other as if there were no tomorrow.

For all we knew, there would not be.

I pulled away from her and looked at the shadow of her image lying below me in the darkness. She pulled her shirt over her head, I buried my face there and inhaled deeply. Her scent drove me mad.

Camira moaned and kissed the top of my head as my mouth found her right nipple. I took it into my mouth lovingly, my tongue licking gently as I sucked. She began to pant with pleasure, and I felt my penis growing hard. I wanted to taste all of her.

I began to move my mouth down her stomach, and she eagerly began to press me down further, helping me along. It made me smile as I kissed her; she had always loved this, and it turned me on even more. I buried my face between her legs and tasted her sweetness, making her moan with delight.

I used my tongue gently, then vigorously, then gently again, pulling back every now and then to drive her mad.

I knew after ten minutes that I would not be able to last at that pace, but I continued, struggling to maintain until she cried out and arched her hips, grinding herself against my face.

I wasted no time in mounting and entering her then. After only a few short strokes I lost complete control. My body went rigid, and I emptied myself into her fully. Camira wrapped her legs and arms tightly around me, caressing me with love as I became spent, and I collapsed on top of her, breathing heavily.

"Oh, Dyzek, I needed that so much!" She let out a giggle and rose to clean herself up and dress. I opened my eyes just as she turned on the dim lamp at her bedside. She stood, and I took in her beauty in all of its glory.

"Me, too," I said simply. "With all that was going on it seemed that I lost touch with the...more important things."

This made her laugh heartily. "I would say you have been focusing on what is important. But we have to remind ourselves what it is we are fighting for, yes?"

"Absolutely, my love." I said adoringly with a smile.

She sat on the bed next to me, and her scent filled my nostrils. How I adored her! She began to stroke my hair, and I began to doze off. The last thing I was aware of was

Camira covering me with the blankets and her warm body snuggling next to mine.

That was what the government was taking from us: our bliss, our happiness, our peace of mind. All things that made life worth living were what they were attempting to steal, and I would not give any of it up without a fight. I would struggle against the machine that consisted of the Elite Marmarans and the Washans. I would kill anyone who got in the way of saving my family: Camira, Barsam, and Morgayne.

No, they would succeed in taking nothing, and if I had my way they would all die before any of us did.

CHAPTER 13

Morning arrived, and while we were all in slightly better spirits, there was still an air of tension about things. Camira and I dressed and had our morning meal just as Morgayne and Barsam were returning home from their tasks. They grabbed their own food and joined us for a brief moment.

"How did things go for the two of you last night?" Camira broke the silence.

"Well," Barsam replied, "all I can say is nothing feels the same."

Morgayne remained silent. I felt the same way, and I knew my partner did as well. The fact was that life would never feel, and would never be, the same.

"I am looking forward to my day," I interjected, trying to be as positive as possible, even though I was a nervous wreck. "I want to get started and find the teleporter."

Barsam knit his brow. "Are you sure you are feeling alright about all of this?"

"It isn't something I have a choice about, Barsam," I said in a serious tone. "Next foot forward."

I stood and wiped my mouth with my napkin and cleared my dishes, with Camira on my heels. When we returned from the food preparation room Camira said, "If either of you need anything, let me know. You know how to reach me."

"Thank you," said Morgayne. "Have as good a day as possible."

∞

The transport to our respective tasks was highly uneventful, boring even. I appeared calm on the outside, but my heart was pounding, and the hairs on the back of my neck stood at rapt. I would begin my search with the closest unmarked section to my task location. I had assigned a letter to each location, 'A' through 'E', and the first, of course, was 'A'.

Location 'A' was only two buildings from mine and was openly used to maintain and store computerized data information for the whole of Marmara. Most of the employees there were Elite Marmarans; the rest were Washans.

According to the map, this building had a massive section of underground floor. The manual's map also had no marking for the section, only a tiny code, which was meaningless. Every section had such a printed code, and the numbers corresponded correctly; it was supposed to be there, the government used them to accurately catalog all places in Marmara.

But there were no clarifying words or terms on the map to tell anybody in any way what this huge section was exactly. Nothing like 'Storage Area', or even 'Washan Living Quarters'. It was just a significant amount of space that seemed to be used for nothing.

It would be easy enough for me to get down there. I was merely going to march on down like it was the most normal thing in the world. I would go on my lunch break and look as official as possible. According to the map, there was a door about thirty feet into the entry corridor, the first door you came to, which led directly down a flight of utility stairs and into the basement. The area would be easy to get to from there.

The only issue that might come up would be if there was someone else in the main corridor. If it was during the regular day shift, I should have no problem blending in and accessing that door.

Plan in mind, I went about my morning, struggling to focus on my computer terminal. My nerves were frazzled, and it was a job to keep it from showing. All in all, I was being torn in every direction possible emotionally, but I could not afford to lose focus.

So the minutes passed, and finally, it was time for the midday meal break. I simply stood and, taking a folder of papers under my arm, headed out of my station and made my way for the main door.

We were given half an hour for our midday meal, and we were permitted to walk, take our food at the park, or run other personal errands, as long as we returned on time. Returning late was never a good thing for Mids since it made them appear to always 'have something up their sleeves'. The government was petrified of rebellion after the first segregation, but they had so many people believing that it was all for their own good.

I reached the record building on foot in no time, and taking a deep breath I grasped the handle to the main door and swung it open.

The corridor was long and narrow and dimly lit. There was a female worker heading out the door, and she did nothing more than smile at me in greeting. I began to walk the thirty feet to the basement door.

The door at the far end of the corridor opened then,

and a male Washan, about my age and dressed in the clothing of the Elite, began to walk toward me. He took notice of me right away, and I nodded and smiled in his direction. But he maintained eye contact, even as he passed me.

"Excuse me, sir, do you work in this building?" I heard that his footsteps had stopped, and my body had tensed. It was right then that I went on autopilot.

I turned on my heel and replied. "Yes, sir, I've been appointed for a bit of light filing duty at basement storage." I opened the file of papers under my arm. The top page was one of the maps, and choosing a room number on the opposite side of the basement from my goal, I looked him in the eye and said, "Section B42."

"Oh," he said, then lifted his eyebrows. "You would have gotten there much faster if you had taken entrance D, but you can get there through that door there." He pointed in the direction of the entrance I was aiming for.

"Thank you, sir. I'll keep entrance D in mind in case I ever return to the building for duty." I gave him another smile and headed for the door.

As I closed it behind me, I had to stop and take a breath. I was sure he could see my heart beating through my chest, but he gave me no sign that he suspected anything. I was here; I could calm down and breathe. With that, I started down the steep set of stairs before me.

The map clearly said that I was in a mid-point in the basement between where I told the man I was heading and where I was really going. If I took a right at the bottom of the stairs, I would find the large section at the very end of that walkway. It would be about a quarter span down the way.

I took a right. There was no one in front of me or behind me, and the only sound I could hear was that of a computer entry device clear at the far end of the hall from where I was heading. I allowed myself to breathe.

At the very end of the hall, was a door with a sign on it. I walked to it, my heart pitter-pattering faster. Maybe I had gotten lucky. Perhaps I had found the teleporter right away!

But as I neared the door, I began to read the sign. It clearly stated, in black letters on yellow:

Sector 3 of 3

Building Materials

So, I hadn't found it after all.

But I wasn't going to not have a look. I grabbed the handle of the door and casting one last glance behind me,

I turned the knob. It wasn't locked, and the door opened.

I was greeted with darkness as black as pitch itself. Instinctively I reached my hand to the buttons which would be located on the wall just inside. Sure enough, they were there, and I pressed the one on top.

The room flooded with light. I looked around the area and realized I could not see the other side. The area was about ten feet in height, and it was packed from top to bottom with tents of black, folded up neatly to save space. There were also countless barrels, each containing long metal rods with spiked ends: the support poles. Here were the 'building materials' used to 'construct' '3 of 3'.

My heart sank, though I had expected disappointment; this room had been way too easy to get to. The teleport unit would be highly guarded when I did find it. I was foolish to even entertain the idea that it might be otherwise.

I reached up and turned the light off, then shut the door behind me. I straightened my shoulders and began my walk back to my task site. A glance at my timepiece told me I had ten minutes to spare. I would stroll.

My return brought me no suspicious looks or nervous questions; it seemed as though no one even noticed I was absent. Since my next opportunity to investigate location

'B' would not be until tomorrow, I was able to focus on my tasks and raise my daily productivity level. I would note what I found directly on the map section, later that evening, at home.

The only distraction left that day was the pending set of segregation announcements that evening. Something inside me told me to relax; all of our regularly assigned tasks were approved the night before. Surely the government wouldn't have someone they intended to segregate report to their tasks? Or would they?

I put it out of my mind and worked the afternoon away.

∞

"Good evening, and greetings to all Marmara! Tonight we will cover tomorrow's temperatures and weather, followed by approved task assignments for tomorrow. The first set of names to be relocated to Sector 3 of 3 will follow. I am sure you are all very excited to see who will move to their new homes!"

The evening announcements had begun, and all of us were quite literally on the edge of our seats. The anxiety in the air could be cut with a knife, and none of us could care less about tomorrow's weather. It was even difficult to get through the task assignments, but the truth was when we all realized we were assigned, we knew none of us would be on the relocation list that night.

All four of us sat through the segregations anyway. We wanted to make sure we were safe, but we also wanted to know who would be going. We mostly had kept to ourselves all these years, and we were each other's best friends. It just seemed essential that we pay attention, for the sake of those who would be relocated. When it was over, we stood in a group embrace, almost breaking down in tears.

It was going to be a very, very stressful time for everyone.

I expected chaos on some level to result from the goings-on. I had prepared my family for this, making sure they understood that some might go off the deep end when taken from their families and friends. Not only did they understand; they easily remembered things from the first time around. That helped matters.

We also discussed my day, and my exploration of location 'A'. I told them how the room was filled with the very materials that all of '3 of 3' consisted of, and how my heart sank at my discovery. It only made sense that it wasn't marked on the map; they probably weren't even using it when the manuals were produced.

So we talked about how that could be the case with all the locations. I highly doubted it though. Something inside of my being told me that the teleporter was in one of the sections we had narrowed down. Almost all marked locations on all the maps coincided with modern use perfectly; the five on our list had been the only questionable ones.

Whether today bred doubts or not, I would continue forward. Each day we were called to tasks was a day of safety so we would press on, and even if all of the remaining four locations proved false, I would keep going until I found it. That was how my mind was set, and that was how it would be.

We would enjoy each minute of our lives as they were together, and we would not stop until we were dead or free.

CHAPTER 14

Location B, the second location I would be investigating, was about four city blocks from my task site. It was a storage building that had no regular task supervisors; according to the manual, sites such as this were only patrolled a few times a day by Elite patrol supervisors. The problem was making good time getting there and back; I would have to make excellent time both ways, as I would with all the remaining locations. The distances grew greater with each destination.

The manual maps said that the building consisted of two above-ground levels, and two that were below ground, each the same measurement as the two above. The top two floors were office space for government offices, and no one worked there but the Elite. While one could access the building easily enough, they could not get into actual work areas without proper credentials, which I didn't want to do anyway.

I wasn't even interested in the first lower level; the maps told us it was nothing but medical storage, and I knew this to be true. Medical equipment had always been there, at least since I could remember. It was no big deal. It was the second lower level, the entire thing, which was completely unmarked.

I would be investigating it during my midday mealtime on the second day of the task week. Since the building housed offices, I would wear a tie to my tasks that day. Once again, I was concerned about blending in. All Elite office workers wore neckties, even the females, on a daily basis.

The second lower level was made up of many different rooms, six to be exact, and each of them was reasonably large, except for a set of restrooms and a maintenance closet. None of the six rooms were marked on the maps, but we counted it as one area in our notes.

So, on the morning of the second day of the task week, I had my breakfast and Camira and I said our goodbyes to our friends before leaving for the day. Their tasks had gone well, and both were in good spirits when we left the house to go to our own. We caught our transport and kissed goodbye when we parted ways.

Today I found I was nowhere near as nervous as I had

been the previous day. I thought it was likely due to settling into reality a bit, but also because I knew Location B would be mostly stress-free, at least until I entered the second lower level and the unknown.

But I was determined, and pushed it out of my mind and carried out my daily tasks as usual. In no time, it seemed, they announced the midday meal break, and without a second thought I stood and grabbed my cloak, walking out the main entrance without even a backward glance.

I walked at a bit more of a rapid pace than the day before, due to the distance, but regardless I made the jaunt in just over seven minutes. I wasted no time in entering the building and making my way to the lift unit, which I rode to the second lower level. When the door opened, I braced myself, but there was no one on the other side.

Once again I entered a long corridor. I looked to the left and the right. Flanking the lift unit past the restrooms, one for each of the sexes, just as the map had said. Right past the men's restroom, to the left of the corridor, was the maintenance room. I found it and breathed a sigh of relief as I made my way to it. I intended for this to be my cover if needed.

The door had no lock, and I turned the knob and ducked into the darkness inside. I allowed my hands to run along the wall until I felt the lighting buttons, which I pushed, flooding the small closet-sized room with light. It would be perfect, as long as I could get to it between searching the other rooms.

According to the map, there would be one more room to the left of where I stood. It didn't look too large, and I planned to start there. There would be four more unidentified rooms on the opposite side of the corridor, and finally, the sixth would be on the other side of the women's restroom. I would work my way around the corridor to my left.

As I prepared to exit, I heard voices outside the door. I instinctively pressed the lighting button and crouched down on the floor next to a water pail. I immediately scolded myself; I should pretend to be utilizing maintenance equipment rather than hiding in the dark like a rat! Well, it was too late.

The voices came closer. "Are you going to be working back down here after your midday meal?" It was a woman, and from the tone of her voice, I could tell she was flirting: her voice dripped honey.

"No, I am done down here for the day," a man replied. His voice seemed to be directly outside the door, and my heart leaped in my chest. I held my breath.

"Well," said the woman, "maybe we could eat together, and you could walk me to my station."

Suddenly the knob rattled on the closet door! I tried to crouch even lower, but I knew it was pointless. "Let me just throw these wrappers away. I had a couple of snacks to tide me over."

Suddenly the door opened, but rather than the light coming on or someone entering, a man's hand went through the lighted crack and dropped fluttering paper into the air. It danced its way to the floor as the door swung shut and clicked solidly closed.

"So why didn't you ask me to lunch before?" the man was asking as his footsteps grew distant. I heard her muffled reply, and flirtatious laughter as the lift doors opened, then closed, and they were gone.

I let out my breath in a massive huff, and my heart seemed to kick-start itself into proper function. I allowed my rear end to rest on the floor, and I got control of myself, standing and listening. I could hear a pin drop, it was so quiet.

Finally, I cracked open the door, squinting against the light. I looked up and down the length of the corridor, but all was clear, so I stepped out and looked to my left.

Sure enough, there was a door. A white sign was fastened to it which read "Clothing Storage and Requisitions: Washan Sectors".

This door had a lock, but it was a simple knob lock which was easily opened with a long, slender object. In my pocket, I had a clip used for joining papers. I always had two or three on me while on task, and with a few simple bends, I knew one of them would be ideal.

Soon I was opening the door and letting the corridor light shine inside. There was a desk with a chair, and a computer for storing orders for clothing and inventory sat on top. Boxes of brand-new garments were piled on either side of it, and garments—tops, bottoms, undergarments, and shoes—either hung or sat neatly folded on shelves. Yes, it was nothing more than clothing storage for the dirty Washans.

I locked the door and closed it behind me, then turned to the first door across the corridor. "Dry Goods and Canned Food: Washan Sectors". It seemed this floor was dedicated to the care of the Washans.

I looked at my timepiece. Lord, I only had eight minutes! I sprinted the few feet to the lift and called it to me, and soon I was on the street, walking as fast as I could back to my own task site. I removed my cloak and sat at my desk with only thirty seconds to spare, and my heart was pounding uncontrollably. After I calmed myself, I looked around. No one was giving me a second look.

Tuesday and one room in Location B down. I would return there tomorrow and make much better time, and I would be sure to bring tools that would make it easier to get into a stronger lock. I was sure I would need them.

Impending Earth

CHAPTER 15

"So, Dyzek, how did it go today?" We were seated at our dining table together, all four of us, just beginning to enjoy our evening meal, which consisted of a thick poultry stew and lots and lots of vegetables. I got tired of the food provided by the computers and food prep units the government controlled. Our meals were frequently bland or unidentifiable.

"It was good," I replied, running my utensil through my food. "I ventured into location B, and while I can't say for sure, it looks like it may be promising."

Camira spoke up. "What did you find?"

"Well, so far I have only looked in one of six rooms, and it was storing Washan clothing. There was also a desk, so I assume it is where they pass out clothes as needed."

I took a bite and quickly washed it down to rid my

mouth of it; it had no flavor, and the salt I'd added had done nothing to improve the situation. I then continued, "The second door said that the room held dried and canned food staples, but I didn't have time to go in; I had to get back to my station." I scooped up a spoonful of the thick stew and let it drip in clumps back into the bowl. "I wonder how much better their food is. If it sounds good, I am taking some of it tomorrow."

"Dyzek!" Morgayne's voice was stern, causing me to look up right away. She was always so soft-spoken, so she easily got my attention. "Why does it look promising?"

I put my spoon in my bowl and wiped my mouth. "It seems the area may be dedicated to the Washans. I don't know about the teleporter, but if we're lucky, I will find something that will lead me in the right direction. Best of all, it doesn't seem heavily manned at all."

"I wouldn't be surprised if all you find is a single guard when the teleporter is found. It won't be used until the end, you know," Barsam said.

I nodded and thought about his words. "You are likely very correct, my friend. I am hoping to at least find something, anything, that refers to it or its use." I took a drink of milk. "It will not be used until needed, I expect, as they would want to be around to see the final segregations through to the end."

Camira joined in. "Just hope it is true because I believe you could handle ridding us of the hassle of a single guard. Don't you?"

"Easily," I replied, nodding curtly to drive the point home. "I am not concerned with who I need to eliminate. If I find the teleporter, it is ours."

We cleaned up the much-wasted meal and made our way for the announcements: day two of the task week, so no segregation list tonight.

As usual, the announcements for the evening were perfunctory and phony, to say the least. The weather would be sunny and wind free. All four of us would be expected at our daily tasks. The same old stuff, only it was beginning to sound more and more rehearsed and plastic.

I was finding it very difficult to take my mind off the teleporter and our plans to escape Marmara. Even though I wanted to be mentally present when I was with those I cared about, it was hard to concentrate. My participation in even the simplest of conversations was basically monosyllabic, and Camira continued to try to pull me in. That night, after we turned into our room, she decided it was time to talk about it.

"Dyzek, I know you have a lot on your mind," she

began. "We all do. Just try to realize that Morgayne is an emotional mess anyway, and when you are so distant from us while at home, it only adds to her stress."

I listened, and answered, half-heartedly. "I know. It is harder than you think to not ponder the situation constantly when our lives are literally at stake." Her correction frustrated me. All the other three really had to do was hope and pray to the gods that I would be successful in my ventures. They didn't really have to do anything or see anything through.

"I am not expecting you to be perfect," she continued. "I am only asking that when you are at home, you try to act more…normal. One could cut the tension with a knife, Dyzek."

I sat up on the edge of the bed and put my head in my hands. I was beginning to feel angry; what did she expect from me?

"You know, Camira, I go to my tasks every day, with a productivity quota that must be met, and all I can think about is what I am going to be doing on my midday meal break," I said, growling a bit in her direction. "I worry over timing, whether or not I will be discovered, what is happening back at home, the quasar, the segregation. Then I take my break and pray that all will go well. I am looking for something in the dark. You, though, you want me to come home and act; act like I am attending a damn tea party!"

"Dyzek, no—"

I interrupted her and continued. "I think it would be more appropriate for all three of you to show a bit more concern. For all of us, for me, for the situation!"

I paused and saw hurt within my lover's eyes. "I love you Camira, and I love Barsam and Morgayne. We are family, and I need your undiluted support."

She grew quiet and did not offer any reply. I had never raised my voice with her, so I knew that she was shocked by my tone. It didn't matter to me right then; I needed her to understand my own state of mind. I needed their support, not their criticisms.

I lay back down and pulled my blankets up under my chin. Camira turned off the lamp next to the bed, casting darkness over the entire room. "Good night, Dyzek," she said in a low tone, and then all was still.

I closed my eyes against the darkness, and my mind went back to the second lower level of the building, and the five rooms I would be investigating. I thought about the canned goods room, and the knob on the door which had nothing more than a basic pop lock, just like the one on the room with the Washan clothing. I was sure that, with that type of lock, the room contained precisely what the sign said it did. If it were more, such as a teleport device or anything related, certainly there would be better protection guarding it. If not a living patroller, at least a more heavy-duty lock.

Camira had given me a small goat-skin purse, about the size of my hand, which contained metal tools with small shelled handles. The tools were created to take care of and maintain the nails on the hands and feet. They were different shapes and sizes, and it would prove to be an excellent resource for picking a lock if I needed to. I believed I would. Surely the Washans wouldn't make it so simple to access the precious teleport. I was anxious to search the rest of those rooms; I had a delicious feeling about this location.

I ended up tossing and turning for some time, thinking and rethinking all of the information I had so far. I fretted over how to cut back on my travel time to the building during my break. I worried over how I would handle running into someone on the second lower level. Finally, I fell into a restless sleep that I seemed to wake up from every hour on the hour.

∞

I woke before Camira the next morning and showered

and dressed quietly. By the time I made my way to the dining area, she was already there, dressed and prepared to begin her own day.

"Good morning, Dyzek," she greeted me over her steaming beverage. "I hope you are feeling well."

I sat down and looked at her, searching for her eyes. "Yes, I'm fine," I replied. "Camira, I…"

She shook her head and held her palm up, gesturing for me to be still. "Don't think on it," she said. "Just try to have a good day. Do you want to eat?"

"Actually I think I am going to pass today," I told her. "My stomach is a bit nervous. I just want you to know that I have a very good feeling about Location B."

She refilled her cup and sat back down. "I am glad, and may my prayers be cast unto you, love."

"It seems that the level I am on is dedicated entirely to the Washans, as I said. The more I think about it, the more convinced I am that I am very close."

"We can hope," she said quietly, smiling at me with loving eyes.

The main door opened, and I heard the voices of Morgayne and Barsam. They were returning home from their tasks, and from where I sat both of them sounded tired and very ready to sleep. The two of them entered the dining area, and Morgayne continued into the food preparation room and pressed the button on the food prep unit. "What is on the menu today?"

Camira replied. "Choice of dry oat cereal or watery eggs."

Barsam cleared his throat to get Morgayne's attention, then shook his head to refuse food. She poured them both a cup of coffee and brought it to the table, then she turned to me.

"Dyzek, I understand you are carrying a large load for all of us, and I am sorry if I have acted like a whining child," she said.

"No!" I felt my eyes grow wide at Morgayne's apology. Was my emotional distance making my loved ones feel as if they were a burden to me? "Morgayne, it is me, not you! We all need to appreciate where we are right now. Nothing we are going through is easy." I looked around at my friends, holding each of their eyes until they acknowledged my words individually.

"Just be easy on me okay?" They all nodded and smiled.

Camira and I left the house in much better spirits, and I was glad to have cleared the air with all of them. It was not anyone's fault that I was filled with anxiety. No one's but the government's, and of course the Washans', and there was nothing I could do about that. The best course of action was the one being taken, and it was imperative that we all get past our fickle emotions and do the next right thing for our family.

I spent the entire transport ride that morning considering what I would do if confronted while on that second lower level. How would I respond? I certainly couldn't just hide, squatting in a dark maintenance closet. That was insanely suspicious, not to mention unacceptable. I needed to get it solidly set in my mind to act like I belonged there. If someone comes, I should indeed head to that closet, but I need to do something productive while I am in there, so as to quash any suspicion.

My morning tasks went smoothly enough, even though my mind was not devoted entirely to them. I did make more entry mistakes than usual, and found that I had to backtrack several times to repair the damages, but I also discovered that I was not concerned. Hell, we were all going to die anyway, if we didn't make it off Marmara alive. What was the point of being concerned about consequences and penalties at this stage?

∞

It seemed that the midday meal break arrived much more quickly than it had the two previous days. Just as I had done the day before I gave no mind to the others milling around to get to their meal; I just grabbed my cloak, equipped with knives and a nail grooming kit, and made my way to the main entrance. Once again, no one paid me any mind.

A quick look at my timepiece told me I left the building one minute before the mealtime actually began. I strode purposefully in the direction of my target, the four-level office building. I entered, seemingly minding my own business, the folder with maps and papers under my arm, and I pressed the button on the lift. According to the lighted numerals over the lift door, it was coming up from the level I was going to; someone was coming from there.

The door opened, and a tall, muscular female Washan lit from the lift. I knew she was Washan only because of a gold-colored metal symbol affixed to the left breast pocket of her clothing: a rising sun flanked by three stars. All Washans wore this on their clothing.

But she also had patches on her sleeves which told me very clearly that she was a patrol guard. She smiled at me as she got off the lift and headed toward the main entry.

I watched her, and just as the lift doors started to close she turned back to me, her brow knit. The door shut and my heart began to beat hard. Was she suspicious?

As the lift took me down my mind raced. I now assumed she was the woman I'd heard asking the man to lunch when I'd been there yesterday, hiding in the maintenance closet. She was a guard, so there was something down there that she was assigned to keep watch over, and the fact that she was Washan told me she was guarding something that was exclusively theirs.

I told myself that she couldn't possibly know which level I was going to; the lift serviced all four levels. For all she knew, I was an Elite who was delivering documents or meeting with a supervisor for re-assignment. By the time the lift doors opened to let me off on the second lower level, I had myself convinced that the look she gave me was all in my head. Stay calm Dyzek.

I immediately turned left, glancing at my timepiece: I had twenty minutes. I approached the door marked for dried and canned goods and looked the knob over. Yes, it was nothing more than another pop lock, and I would not waste my valuable time opening it, even if I did want to see what they were eating. I backtracked to door number three, and as soon as I read the sign I caught my breath:

Washan Teleport Sciences

and Travel Documentation

UNAPPROVED ENTRY

STRICTLY FORBIDDEN.

I looked down at the doorknob. There was no keyhole. To my shock, it was another simple pop lock. I was so surprised I almost forgot why I was there.

I wasted no more time in digging out my nail grooming pouch, in which I had placed my wire clip for safekeeping. It took a few seconds for me to pop the lock, and the door opened wide as if welcoming me inside. I didn't even have to search for lights; they were already on.

The room consisted of three large cabinets, each taller than I. The cabinets had four drawers in them each, and metal tabs labeled with letters that I didn't recognize marking the contents in Washan alphabet. In the middle of the room were a computer terminal and data entry device; the screen on the terminal was dark, and there was no flashing light signifying that it 'slept'.

I wasted no more time. I would grab what I could and

get out of there. I would take what I found home and replace it the next day. My mind was racing; if I couldn't identify the letters on the drawers, how would I be able to read or translate anything I saw? Then I remembered that Camira knew some of the Washan language. Her task in the nutrition department required that she learn it, which she had done shortly after the first segregations. She could not speak the language, but she could read it.

I went to the first cabinet and pulled open the top drawer. It was filled with large groups of files. Suddenly it occurred to me that I had no time to start at the beginning and go from there, not with the time limits I had. I stood back and looked over the three cabinets, then settled on the third drawer down in the middle one and took the first two files; then, I quickly shut the drawer. Shaking, I went back to the door and set the pop lock as I closed the door behind me. I then went to the lift and pushed the button, tucking the files under my arm with the original one I had brought with me.

No one was on the lift, and in no time I was back on the street, walking back to my own task site. I arrived with minutes to spare and found I could barely settle in or sit still. I was anxious to talk to Camira and see what she had to say. What did the files contain? If nothing else, she could clarify the Washan alphabet so I could possibly narrow down the files I took. I was so excited I could barely contain myself.

Even as I sat at my task station and tried to focus on my work my mind wandered to that room on the second lower level. I knew with as much certainty as I knew my own name that the location of the teleporter was either on that level or would be revealed in the documents kept in that room. I didn't know what the documents I grabbed would tell us, but I did know that Camira would be able to guide me regarding what documents I should grab next, and from what drawer, by the markings on them.

∞

The day dragged on, and it seemed that whenever I checked the time it had barely changed. I went to the restroom more than usual and even had a co-worker ask me if I had a bad coffee habit. I laughed and shrugged off the joke, but I knew I was drawing attention to myself by trying to pass the time. I spent the rest of the afternoon trying to keep my mind on the job before me, and it was anything but easy. My productivity suffered far more that day than I would have liked. But I knew that wouldn't matter soon enough.

When the end of the task day finally arrived, I gathered the files and covered them with my cloak, then made my way out to catch the transport. Tonight they would announce the second group of segregates, and I hoped that none of us were on the list. All I wanted was a peaceful evening, one conducive to openly going over the files and gleaning a much-needed education from Camira on the Washan language.

She was on the transport already, I kissed her cheek and smiled at her, and she sighed with relief at the sight of me. I had been so wrapped up in my own anxiety that I hadn't even considered what the stress was doing to those closest to me. I felt terrible, and I made up my mind to apologize to the three of them at supper that evening.

∞

The transport let us out in front of our home, and I took Camira's hand for the short walk to the door. "How did things go today?" she asked without looking at me.

"Very well, I think," I replied cheerfully. "I am anxious to fill all of you in, and I will be needing a bit of your help."

Now she looked right at me. "Mine?"

I couldn't help but laugh at her surprised tone. "Yes,

silly. Yours."

Once inside the house we stopped so Camira could hang her cloak, and I put the files down on a side table next to the sofa in the sitting room. I then took a turn hanging my own cloak before I turned to Camira and our two friends, who were seated in the main area listening to music.

"Good day, friends," I began. "I am ravenous! Does anyone know what our loving caregivers have prepared for our evening meal?"

Barsam rolled his eyes in an exaggerated manner and smiled. "Beef and gravy over potato root," he said. "The basics of survival."

Fortunately, it was one of the better meals we were served, so I was happy. "Well, I am ready to eat, if the rest of you are." With that I made my way into the dining area, the other three hot on my tail.

The girls prepared the four plates while Barsam and I made small talk about his task and how it had been the night before. He reported that his co-workers behaved just as mine did: they acted as though nothing was out of the ordinary, even seeming to be happy and content with the new segregations. "I can barely keep my mind on my tasks during the day, I worry so," he reported. "I don't understand how everyone can act as if nothing is happening at all."

"They are sheep," I stated firmly. "What they do not know causes them no pain, and they genuinely believe the government has their welfare in mind."

The girls appeared, both carrying two plates of food. They set down the plates and returned to the food preparation room to fetch our glasses of cold milk. Once, all four of us were seated comfortably, we had our evening nourishment in silence.

I ate quickly. I was so hungry that it felt as if I hadn't eaten in days. Then I recalled that I had skipped breakfast and lunch, and had likely taken more than my share of coffee for the day. It should have come as no surprise that I gulped my food down like I did. I caught Camira giving me strange looks, to which I responded with nothing more than a smirk and a wink.

In about ten minutes time our plates were all clean, and I had pushed mine away in favor of my milk. I gulped it down, and when I was finished, I saw that my three companions were looking at me with intense curiosity.

"Oh!" I began. "I'm sorry to have taken so long. It seems I couldn't wait to fill my stomach."

Morgayne stood to gather the dishes, but I reached out and touched her arm. "Wait for that, if you would. I have something I need to say."

She looked at Camira as though for approval, and Camira gave her a slight nod and a smile. "I feel as if I should say I am sorry to you all for not considering how you may be feeling during this stressful time. Indeed, I have worries, but no more than you three. Please forgive me."

"Of course, Dyzek," Barsam said immediately. "Now, if you are done with the silliness, what happened today? I saw you had an armload of papers with you."

I smiled at him and stood. "Stay where you are." I fetched the two large files from the table in the main area and returned to the table. "I went back down to the second lower level in the office building," I began. "First, I should tell you that a female guard came up from there for her midday break; I am sure she is posted on that level for security."

"Did she say anything to you?" Camira's voice was filled with concern.

I shook my head. "We only encountered each other as she got off the lift and I got on. I don't think we should be concerned."

I continued. "Anyway, I didn't go into the room marked for food storage. I figured it held exactly what it said, just as the first room had. But the third, well, that is a different story."

I related to them what the sign on the door said, how the room held teleportation information. "It actually read, 'Science and Travel documentation', and while I don't know what that means precisely, I figured it can lead us in the right direction.

"The only problem is that the cabinets that hold the files are all marked with the Washan alphabet, and I am at a loss."

Camira immediately became excited. "I can read it!" She reached for the first file.

"I knew that you could, so I grabbed these two out of the middle cabinet on a whim. Tonight I will need you to show me what you can about the alphabet so I can find more relevant files on the teleporter tomorrow if needed."

I placed my hand over hers as she began to flip through the file. "I think we should wait. Let's view the announcements and put that behind us for the night."

The mood in the room immediately tensed up, but all agreed. We stood and made our way into the main area, where I turned on the screen while the others took their seats. Soon we were listening to the weather predictions for the following day.

"Expect a bit of wet weather tomorrow, with clouds, but you can count on reasonably warm temperatures and little to no wind," the announcer said with a smile. "Aside from the drops of rain, it will be a wonderful day. Please stay in attendance to hear the task approvals for tomorrow, day three of the five-day task week!"

Task announcements were made, and once again we were all expected at work. We stuck around for the segregation report, but it listed no one with whom we were familiar. We had managed to keep to ourselves well over the years in Sector 2.

When the reports were done, and we had all breathed massive sighs of relief at our once again 'narrow escape' we took to the dining room to go over the files which I had brought home.

"Now," I began, holding up my hand to Camira in an effort to slow down her grabbing hands. "There were three cabinets, and each contained four drawers. I took these from the middle of the second cabinet, hoping to find anything that would point us to the location of the teleporter, as well as how to use it."

Camira opened the first file eagerly and began to read to herself. She skimmed and flipped, and even skipped a few pages. After a bit, she stopped. Something grabbed her attention, and she was focused sharply on the paper before her, her eyes growing wide.

"What is it?" Barsam asked.

Camira looked up. "Well, you will be happy to know that so far the documents are all about the teleporter. From what I can see, by the little reading I have done, the Washans have visited countless planets." She turned her attention back to the papers.

"I think it is best if we let her read alone, so she can focus." I touched her lightly on the arm. "Camira, do you need anything? Note paper? Writing utensil?"

She looked up briefly and shook her head before turning her attention back to the job at hand. Barsam, Morgayne, and I returned to the main area. We put the music on low and sat down to converse a bit.

"It seems you may have hit the jackpot, my brother," Barsam told me with a smile on his face. "I knew if anyone could do it, you could."

"I am apprehensive to get my hopes up, but it certainly does appear I am headed in the right direction," I replied. "If so, I will need her to help me with the language, so I can track down the instructions and location of the machine."

Morgayne cleared her throat to let us know she had something to say. "I think it is down on that second lower level."

"I suspect the same," I added, "but we need to be sure, so we are not running around aimlessly, wouldn't you both agree?"

They both nodded at me just as Camira shouted, "I have found something important!"

We jumped up and made our way back into the dining area, where Camira sat with her face glowing.

"I believe I have found the planet they intend to take refuge on, after the destruction of Marmara."

CHAPTER 16

Camira's voice was filled with excitement, and she could hardly wait for us to all be seated before she began.

"The planet, which has no name, is located two entire galaxies from ours," she began. "According to the documents in this second file, which is devoted to information on the planet, there are no living human beings similar to us; all detected life are simple animals."

She looked at each of us, then continued. "They have visited before, but only since arriving here," she said. She then shoved some papers in front of me, but when she realized I could not translate she shook her head and took them back. "It says the planet is nearly identical to ours in all aspects, except for the lack of human life and it is much larger. It is ideal for supporting life, growing food, and thriving."

"This also says they will take only a total of five

hundred Marmarans and Washans to the new location."

I thought on it for only a moment before asking her, "Does it say when they intend to leave?"

Now her face grew serious. "Yes."

I waited, but she did not continue. "Well?"

Now she took a deep breath and looked each of us in the eye, one after the other. "This states that the quasar, which destroyed Washa, is predicted to hit Marmara five weeks from tomorrow. The teleportation will begin three weeks from tomorrow to ensure that all five hundred find safety."

She looked down, and I saw tears well up in her eyes. "There are many Elite that are not being chosen to go. The escape from Marmara has been carefully orchestrated by the Washans. I need a bit of time to read more, but I suspect they have ulterior motives for taking any of us at all."

"What motives?" Barsam sounded confused and nervous.

Camira simply looked at him. "I need another hour, please."

Once more we stood and made our way into the living area to wait. It seemed that, even for the Marmaran government, things were not as they appeared with the Washans. I could only hope that we could find a way out.

∞

For the next hour and a half, Camira sat alone in the dining area reading the files. The three of us were easily nervous wrecks as we waited in the other room for her voice to call out to us. On two occasions I snuck a peek at her, hoping to catch her attention and have her call us, but to no avail.

Barsam and Morgayne were expected to arrive at their tasks an hour before the midnight point. They were already rested, as they slept while Camira and I worked, but I found that I was growing fatigued indeed. I was just beginning to doze off in my chair when Barsam spoke.

"Dyzek, Camira calls," he said urgently.

I jumped up from my seat, suddenly wide awake, and made my way into the dining area. We took our seats and waited, expectantly, for Camira to fill us in on what she had discovered.

"First of all, the teleport unit is located on the second lower level, just as you suspected," she began. "Each joined set of documents here in the first file explains an individual teleport mission, and per legalities for the Washans, they have documented the location of the teleport device they have used, it seems they have more than one."

She began to shuffle through the papers from the first file for effect. "Most of these are missions that took place while Washa was still in existence, with the exception of the second file." She paused and shuffled through it as well. "This is information on the new planet, the one they intend to relocate to, the one we need to access.

"That is the good news," she continued. "There is a planet we will be safe on if only we can learn how to use the device, and then access it successfully without hindrance. But there is bad news."

"What?" I asked with trepidation.

She cleared her throat. "It appears that, by the time the Washans discovered Marmara, they were out of time. They would never have attempted to settle on an inhabited planet; it is not their style, so to speak. Washa was not even originally theirs, from what I am gathering.

"So, as a matter of salvation they came, but it seems they immediately began the dwindling process of our people. They exercised their influence to manipulate and control our government, and they obviously were very, very successful." Now she crossed her arms over her chest, a look of disgust coming over her face. "But as I said, it appears they have a motive we didn't understand."

Barsam's curiosity got the best of him. "For the love of the gods, Camira, out with it!"

She smirked and rolled her eyes. "They are taking only the smartest and best because they want only the finest slaves on their new planet," she said. "Strong builders, breeders, and workers to help them become established for all time."

I stood and began to pace back and forth. "Slaves!?, I knew all of their 'care and concern' was too good to be true."

Camira continued. "It also appears that, once the Washans have built up a sufficient population, they will execute all Marmarans they have taken. No one on this planet is going to survive in the end, if the Washans have their way."

Finally, Morgayne had something to say. "Can't we just take this and show it to the governing authorities?"

"No," I replied quickly. "Even if the government find out the truth and act, they will compromise those of us whom they have come to see as weak. It will make no difference to our current circumstances."

We all fell into silence, thinking about what Camira had just brought to light. The best bet was to continue on as we were planning. I needed to find the instructions to the teleport device, pinpoint the room where it was located, and get my family out of here.

"Does any of that tell us the coordinates to the new planet's location?" I asked Camira.

She nodded. "Of course. Several times on several pieces of paper."

"Okay," I said, "Here is what we will do. Camira, I need you to copy any information pertinent to our cause, including coordinates and which room the teleport device may be in. If you cannot locate that, don't worry. There are only three rooms left on the second lower level. I am confident it is one of them.

"I will also need you to write down the Washan words for 'teleport', 'teleportation', 'instructions', 'directions', and 'operations'. When I return tomorrow I will take back these files, so we need copies of anything important."

"I can do that on our home printing unit tonight," she said enthusiastically.

I continued. "When I go tomorrow I intend to look for a file that is focused only on the device itself, so make sure you give me the proper Washan words to locate it. I believe that is all we can do for now, so it is important that we are thorough, and that we do it all correctly."

So that became the plan. I would take any files related to the actual teleport unit, and we would figure out how to operate the damn thing. The four of us, with Aldan, if possible, would escape Marmara once and for all. We would not be 'Mids' or 'Dregs', and we would certainly not be enslaved by the monsters that called themselves 'Washans'.

Camira and I were still going over the file on the new planet when Morgayne and Barsam left for their tasks. We were up until nearly two hours past the midnight point; we had to force ourselves to get some sleep. The good news was that we had made great strides of discovery, and we had a better-than-average chance at survival—at least, we did in comparison to the rest of Marmara. Only time would tell.

Impending Earth

CHAPTER 17

I sat at the desk at my workstation the next morning thinking about the files Camira had copied, which were now safely tucked away under my cloak. I would return them during my midday meal break, at which time I would attempt to locate instructions on the teleport device. It would also be imperative that I find the device itself, by tomorrow at the latest, as the task week would be drawing to a close. According to what we had learned from the Washan files, we would have only a little over two weeks to make our grand escape.

Once we had these issues narrowed down, the main problem would be how to destroy the teleport device so no one could follow us. From my daily tasks, I was familiar with the defensive weapons we had used at one time on Marmara, and to the best of my knowledge, they no longer existed. But I did know that a museum, located in the center of the Elite sector, it housed a specific type of explosive, for display purposes only, of course. I did a bit of reading on the device, and it clearly stated that it had been rendered powerless, but I was sure we could figure out a way to make it work, if only I could get my hands on it.

As usual, the morning passed at a leisurely pace, and when the time came, I grabbed my files and cloak and made my way to the office complex. I had gotten to the point where I no longer paid attention to my nerves. After what I had learned the previous night, all I felt was fury. If we were going to die, so be it, but we would die fighting to be free! We were on the side of righteousness, and I firmly believed that to be true.

My walk to the office building was uneventful, but when I boarded the lift the female guard was on it, and she made no effort to get off, as she had before. This fact made my heart skip a beat, but I got on it anyway, smiling at her as I did.

I reached out and pushed the button which would take me to the first lower level; she appeared to be going to the second floor, so I was forced to ride with her.

"Have you worked in this building long?" she asked me suddenly. "You seem familiar to me, though I don't recall seeing you before the other day."

I turned to her and flashed my best smile. My, she was a big one, though not unattractive. I was sure that she could beat me to a pulp if the need arose. "I am only doing temporary information entry for the medical supplies being issued to the new sector."

The lie fell from my lips without my even having to think, and she bought it. "Are you as relieved as I am to be getting rid of the leeches being moved to '3 of 3'?" she asked.

"Are you kidding?" I replied. "I thought they would never bring the law to pass."

She gave me a hearty chuckle. "Too bad we are even wasting supplies on the Dregs, but what the powers say is what we do, yes?"

"At all times," I said.

The lift stopped and opened up, and the guard got off. "Have a good day," she offered as she left, and I nodded in response, with a smile, of course.

What pigs the Washans were! How little regard for life they had! To know the real depths of the truth infuriated me beyond words. More than ever, I wanted to leave this planet and all of its nightmarish memories behind.

I pushed the button to the second lower level and then had to go through stopping on the first lower level once more. This ate up more of my time than I would have liked, but at this point, I no longer cared. I got off on the desired floor and walked directly to the room I wanted. In no time I popped the lock and entered the room.

First I replaced the first two files, then I used the translation key Camira had made to locate any records with reference to 'teleport' or 'teleportation'. It turned out to be much easier than I thought it would be. In only minutes I had a file that broke down the device's design, and another which was labeled as operational instructions.

So far, so good.

As I rode the lift back to the main floor, I looked at my timepiece. I would be a couple of minutes late so I would have to feign sickness or something. Hopefully, no one noticed, but I was mentally prepared for any confrontation. At this point, I just wanted to do what it took to ensure the safety of my family.

∞

We were all so anxious to go over the day's findings when I returned home with Camira that night that we couldn't even eat our evening meal. Full plates sat before us, untouched, as Camira began reading through the files.

After about ten minutes she placed a sheet of paper with a map on it before me. "Is this the corridor of the second lower level?" she asked.

No more than a glance told me it was, and I nodded at her with a smile. "There is the maintenance closet, and this is the room with the cabinets where these files are all kept."

She then pointed a tapered finger at the last door on the same side of the corridor. "The teleportation device is located here," she stated firmly.

"Are you sure?" I asked, almost in disbelief.

She nodded. "Positive. According to this, it is typically monitored by a guard who is stationed inside, but only during the task day."

"That would be the big woman I have encountered," I replied. "It is unguarded on the weekends?"

"As far as I can see," she said.

She continued to read them, and we let her be. Announcements would start in twenty minutes, and I thanked the gods it was not a night to hear segregations. I didn't need any more worries than what I had.

At five minutes before announcements, Camira pulled herself away from the files, and we attended our viewing obligations. All of us would attend tasks, and we didn't care about anything else. Priest Klantz gave a half-hearted appreciation speech, thanking all those who were being so cooperative during the relocations. He was proud that there had been no runners, as of yet anyway.

With that behind us, we went back to the table and sat, waiting for any and every word Camira would speak. She mostly kept quiet, though, and the three of us ended up back in the living area viewing the evening's pre-programmed film, which usually we never did. About an hour before Barsam and Morgayne were scheduled to leave, Camira popped her head around the corner.

"I am ready," she said simply.

We lost no time in joining her and sat eagerly waiting for her to fill us in on everything.

"Dyzek, you have done it, my love," she began, "and with much greater speed and success than any of us anticipated. These are the operational instructions for the teleportation device designed by, and owned by, the Washan people."

She began to spread out different sheets on the table, which prompted Morgayne to clear the plates finally. She was back in only moments, at which point Camira continued. "All of the sheets contain different information, all in order and numbered, but each sheet states the location of the teleporter. I assume it is Washan practice to be so consistent."

She pointed at the first sheet. "The instructions are simple: the device teleports only one individual at a time, and they may carry one item with them. It must fit in the parameters given if it is to make it through," she continued. "Before that individual boards, the coordinates are entered…" she pointed to the second sheet. "Here. Then it is as simple as standing back and pressing a button. There is a button for the final traveler, which is located here." She pointed to the third sheet. "This is an internal command module. It should be used only for the final passage, to ensure safe travel to all who go before. The device will be quite warm by then, and it suggests waiting three minutes between travels, though it is not required."

"We are really going to do this, aren't we?" Morgayne asked with a smile.

Camira turned to her. "You bet we are."

Now I spoke. "Before we get too excited we must discuss the destruction of the machine after the last traveler passes. I suggest the explosives on display at the Elite museum," I said. "Tonight we will copy all this, then tomorrow, when I return to the basement with these documents, I will take some of the Washan clothing. That way we can travel amongst them easily, both to get the explosive and to get to the device when it is time."

I knew the plan needed to be polished, and I had time to do that. For now, Barsam and Morgayne had to leave, and Camira and I had much copying to do. I could only hope we had enough paper to get the job done.

So our night, until just after mid-point, was spent entirely on printing copies of the files I had brought. Camira made sure that the documents I needed to operate the teleport were all together, and she put all the rest with the previous copies we made. If worst came to worst, we would have proof to show our own government in the case we needed to plead for our lives.

We had teased about making love that night, but we both fell into a deep sleep as soon as our heads touched the pillows. I dreamed of it, though. In my dream, Camira and I made carefree love under a tree of green and a sky of blue. There were no tents where we were and no designated sectors for those who were considered 'less'. It was us in a perfect world, a little piece of heaven all our own.

I woke with a start to her shaking me. At first, I was angry that she had pulled me from my Utopia, but then I realized it was time to start a new day, and carry out the next steps of our risky plan to save our lives. I put my feet on the floor and trudged to the shower.

As the hot water hit me in the face and ran over my body, I realized how far we had come since this started. At any moment we would inevitably run into resistance. While I needed to be ready for it, I knew it wouldn't matter. No one would be able to stop us at this point. Either I would die, or they would die in their efforts. It was all past discussion now.

Impending Earth

CHAPTER 18

"Dyzek, can I see you for a moment?" It was my cousin Maron standing at the door of my task station, his arms crossed before him, a serious look on his face.

I stood. "Sure, Maron. What can I do for you?"

He entered, so others would know an Elite was talking to a Mid out of necessity. "You arrived back from your midday meal break a bit late yesterday. As you know, I am required to clarify the reason and assess whether or not it is acceptable."

"Of course, Maron, of course," I replied. "I'm not sure if the meat I ate was bad or not, but it made my stomach very queasy. I ended up in the men's restroom for...quite some time. I am not even sure anyone was able to...enter after I was done." I offered him an embarrassed grin and sheepish look.

Maron let out a massive sigh of relief and rolled his

eyes as he began to laugh. "I know you are aware that you should let us know right away when you are late for any reason," he said. He wiped his hand across his forehead. "I can understand why you were hesitant, so I will cover for you. Are you better today?"

"I was better almost immediately yesterday, thank you, Maron," I replied.

He stood and put his hands in his pockets. "I'm sorry to put you on the spot in such a way. Carry on. I will fill in the upper heads regarding your…reasons."

We both laughed together, and Maron left my station. I wanted to scream. My hands were shaking, and I had broken out in a sweat, but somehow I had convinced him. I had never been a liar, and it struck me as funny how many lies I had convincingly told in the recent past. I hoped I would not have to continue this way.

I sat at my entry device and placed my hands on it, but for a moment my fading fear and nervousness did not even allow me to move. I closed my eyes and took a few deep breaths. I could not afford to be even a few seconds late today, and I needed to grab Washan uniforms. There would be no time to check sizes or anything else. It would be a rushed job for sure.

Tonight, the third set of segregates would be announced. I could only pray to the gods that we received the same mercy we had been getting; otherwise, we would be hiding away until we could get to the machine. If even one of our names was announced, it could spell disaster, and we all knew that full well. Even the thought of collecting Aldan frightened me to death, but a promise was a promise.

Midday meal came quickly, probably because of my fear. Before it was even announced, I had grabbed my cloak and the files and began to mosey, albeit nonchalantly, to the main entrance. Even a few seconds of extra time would help. I was determined to not waste any time, and made my way there at a breakneck pace, often looking at my timepiece as if I were late already, all for appearance's sake.

When I entered the main area, the big female was just getting off the lift. I nodded at her, and she smiled in response. That's what 'early' gets me, I thought to myself as I got on the lift and pressed the button; running head-on into those I wanted to avoid. I needed to think things through more carefully if I expected our plan to succeed.

As usual, the basement's second level was completely empty and quiet. I had my wire clip ready in my pocket, and I proceeded to open the door to the room holding the file cabinets. I then replaced the two thick files with the teleport information. For a split second, I found myself concerned about not putting them into their proper places, but I forced myself to put the thought out of my mind. I just didn't have time to dally.

Next, I left the room, popping the lock securely behind me. I made my way across the hall to the Washan clothing room, and once inside I quickly grabbed four full-body jumpsuit-type tunics. I paid no attention to size or color. I only got what I needed, wrapped them securely in my cloak, and left the room, once again making sure the lock was popped, and the door was secured.

I glanced at my timepiece and discovered I was actually a bit ahead of schedule. Perfect. I wanted to get an eyeful of the door which covered the room to the teleportation device. It was across the hall on the opposite end, so I jogged down there and read the large sign on the door. It was red with large white lettering.

WASHAN ACCESS ONLY!

ABSOLUTELY <u>NO</u> ADMITTANCE

UNLESS ACCOMPANIED BY

HIGH-LEVEL WASHAN AUTHORITY

This was it! This was the room which housed the sacred teleportation device we so badly needed to access.

I had found it!

I looked down at the lock on the door. It was not a simple pop lock, but rather, it required a key card, much like the ones used to enter our homes. My heart sank. How was I going to solve this issue? I could not begin to figure out how I would get my hands on any key card that would get me inside.

Right then I heard the lift activate, and it was clearly coming down. Panicked, I headed directly for the maintenance closet. I took the bundle that held the Washan clothing and tucked it behind a large rubbish bin. Then, with shaking hands, I began to fill a cleaning pail with water. It was all I could think of to do to look inconspicuous.

I heard the lift doors open then, and right away it was followed by the sound of shoes on the stone floor. I was straining to hear clearly over the sound of the running water, but at first, I could have sworn the footsteps were heading away from me. Then they stopped, and when they resumed, I knew they were coming toward the very closet which I was in.

My heart was pounding nearly out of my chest as I turned off the water. Right then the doorknob began to turn, and the door to the maintenance closet swung open.

Before me stood the female guard who I had encountered the last few days on the lift, and she looked stunned.

"What are you doing down here?" she sneered, the pleasant smile I had seen replaced with a look of anger and suspicion. "This level is strictly open to Washans only, as I am sure you know!"

I cleared my throat and offered her a smile of my own. "A mess was made in the level above, in medical storage," I offered. "There was no pail, so I was going to borrow this one."

She looked at the water-filled pail and then back at me, apparently unsure of whether or not to believe the motive I offered her. "That doesn't matter," she said after a moment. "You are not to be on this level, for any reason."

My hands were trembling violently, and I was keeping them behind me, somewhat so she would not notice. With my right hand, I clutched one of the knives which was concealed in the pocket of my trousers, mostly just to make myself feel more secure. Just as my fingers curled around its handle, the large woman spat, "You are going to have to come with me!"

Suddenly she had a painful grip on my upper arm, and she was jerking me out of the closet. I tried to pull away, but she held fast, and my resistance seemed to anger her even more. My brain was going more quickly than I could keep up with, and panic was threatening to take over completely.

"I need to get the pail upstairs," I said, trying to free myself from her grasp. The woman was large, though, and the small space I was in did not afford me the room to put up the struggle I needed to free myself. In seconds she had me out in the hall, and I began to put up a fight in full.

She slung me against the corridor wall with great force, and I hit it and slid to the floor. I was trying to stand when she came at me, partially tackling me to keep me on the floor. What happened next happened so fast I barely even understood it until it was over.

She began to hit me in the side of my head, so hard that lights were flashing in my eyes. I tried to hit her with my left, but it didn't even faze her. So I swung my right, hitting her full-on in her left side. Her eyes grew very wide, and her mouth flew open. She looked at me, confused, and the look confused me as well. Suddenly she crumbled to the floor.

I could only stare at her, my mind trying desperately to figure out how my single blow had taken the woman down so easily. I looked down at my hand, and that was when I saw the knife in it, and the blood that covered it. I had stabbed the guard in the side of her head.

I dropped the knife to the floor and looked at her face. A gurgling sound crept from her throat and persisted, and it was soon followed by a stream of blood, which ran from her mouth, down her cheek, and began to pool on the floor next to her head. Her wide eyes looked at me as though she expected me to help her, and her mouth moved as though she wanted to ask for aid but could not. I only sat there and stared. After a moment her eyes grew distant, and I heard her breathe her last.

I must have been holding my breath because when I exhaled, it was a great relief. I looked the woman up and down, my mind on overdrive. I had murdered a Washan guard! What was I going to do? I was no longer thinking about the time or being late returning to my task site. Now I was looking around anxiously, trying to figure out my next move.

"Breathe, Dyzek, breathe," I said out loud, and forced myself to inhale and exhale slowly. Once I had calmed myself a bit, I stood. I had to move this body. I had to get it out of sight and clean up the mess.

I went into the closet and grabbed the bundle that was wrapped up in my cloak. I took the Washan garments into the corridor and set it safely down at the end, near the door to the clothing room from where I got them. Then I returned to the closet and grabbed the pail full of water out of the large floor basin, along with an armload of cleaning towels from the shelf next to it. I took those into the corridor and set them down next to the guard's lifeless body.

I would move her body into the maintenance closet and leave it there. I would clean up the blood, take the clothing, and get out of here as quickly as possible. I grabbed her by the arm and began to pull her across the floor, and that was when I took note of the card which hung from a long cord around her neck.

A key card.

I immediately stopped and removed it, and without another thought walked to the room I believed held the teleport device. I swiped the card, and the red light, which indicated that the door was locked, turned green. The door popped open.

The room was fully lit, and a great hum filled the air. There was nothing in the room but a booth, large enough for a single person to stand in. It was constructed of glass, or some other clear, hard material, and there were all kinds of lights flashing on the machine. Next to it was a pedestal with a panel on it, and the board was filled with buttons and switches.

I was in. It was that simple. But now was not the time to let my curiosity get the best of me. It was vital that I finish the job right. I backed out of the room, literally having to force myself to get back to the body. The door latched shut and locked on its own, and I tucked the key card safely into my trouser pocket, with my other knife. Then I made my way back to the woman and finished dragging her body into the closet.

There was a pretty good pool of her blood on the corridor floor, and dragging her had smeared a full trail across the floor. I cleaned it with the towels and water, then dumped out the bucket and threw the wet, bloody towels into the rubbish bin. I tried to hide her body best I could, but naturally, there was no way in the tiny closet. Finally, I shut the door and made sure it was securely latched. I leaned back against it and allowed myself to breathe while I looked myself over; I appeared to be blood-free.

Then reality hit me, and I looked at my timepiece. My heart sank. I was a half-hour late for my task. How was I going to explain myself? What was I going to do?

I concluded that it didn't matter at this point. I would take the things I had gathered—the Washan clothing and the key card— and I would return home. I would notify my supervisor that the illness which had stricken me earlier in the week had come on full force, and I did not want to risk infecting others. I would then contact Camira and let her know I would not be on the transport home that afternoon so she would not worry herself.

Impending Earth

CHAPTER 19

Calmed and collected, I fetched my cloak, which held the clothing and got on the lift. The strangest sense of calm came over me, and as I rode up to the main level I began to hum a tune, and a smile came over my face. Nothing mattered now; we were on the horizon of success. I would not feel guilty, nor would I worry about any consequences for my actions with the dead guard.

As I left the office complex, no one paid me any mind at all. I caught the next transport going in the direction of my home, and when I arrived, I called on my cousin Maron. I put on the sickest-sounding voice I could muster as he picked up his line.

"Maron, it is Dyzek," I began.

"Dyzek!" he replied, a bit of anger in his voice. "Where are you? Do you not know the kind of trouble you are in?"

I cleared my throat for effect. "Maron, I am sorry. It seems I am very ill. I am running a high fever, and began vomiting during my meal break." I threw in a couple of coughs for good measure.

"Is it the sickness from before, do you think?" he asked.

I took a ragged breath. "I am not sure, but I don't want to pass it around."

"No! Absolutely not!" he replied. "Get some rest. It is the last day of the week, after all. I will make sure to speak with your direct supervisor right away. I am sure I can smooth over his anger."

"Thank you, Maron," I said. "I am going to take a remedy and go right to bed."

"Hopefully we see you next week," he said, wrapping up the conversation. "Get well, Dyzek."

I coughed once more. "Thank you." Then I disconnected.

I turned around to take the Washan clothing out of my cloak and get a good look at my plunder. That was when I noticed Barsam standing there watching me, his hair mussed from sleep.

"I am sorry if I woke you, Barsam," I said.

He shook his head. "It was time for me to rise anyway," he replied. "What are you doing here, Dyzek?"

"Well," I began, "I hit a bit of a snag today, and was unable to return to work."

"What happened?" he asked, a concerned look on his face.

I held up my hand. "Give me a moment," I said. I had suddenly remembered I needed to contact Camira, which I did. While she wanted details, I put her off, telling her I was 'ill' and would fill her in when she got home. Appeased, she disconnected, and I turned my attention back to Barsam.

"I went to the office complex for the Washan clothing today," I said, holding up one of the outfits. "I found the room with the teleporter, but it required a key card for entry."

Barsam sat down hard, a sad look on his face. "What are we going to do?"

"Nothing," I replied. I took the stolen key card from my trouser pocket and waved it before him.

He jumped up. "Where did you get that?" he asked.

Now it was my turn to sit. Suddenly I felt overwhelmed with exhaustion. The events of the midday break were catching up to me, I knew. I had dealt with some very tumultuous circumstances and had not given myself the time to cope with my emotions at all. I put my elbows on my knees and my head in my hands.

"Just as I was getting ready to leave the level, the guard came down the lift," I began.

Morgayne's voice spoke from the hallway. "Oh, my God, are you okay?"

I looked up, a bit startled at her sudden appearance, then I nodded and continued. "Yes. I went into the maintenance closet and pretended to fill a pail with water, but she came in and began to question me. I told her I needed it for a mess on the next level, but she didn't care. She grabbed me and attempted to detain me."

Morgayne sat down. "How did you break free?"

I took a deep breath and sat back, closing my eyes. "I killed the guard with my knife," I said nervously.

Both of them jumped to their feet, stricken looks covering their faces. "Oh!" said Morgayne, her hands flying up and covering her mouth.

"Dyzek, my friend," Barsam began, "are you okay?" He sat down next to me and draped his arm over my shoulders. That was all it took, the physical contact of my dear friend. At his touch, I broke down sobbing, crying tears like a child. Morgayne and Barsam remained still, allowing me to cry as I took comfort in their silence.

When my tears were spent, I wiped my eyes with the back of my hand, then rose to clear my sinuses. When I had myself put together, I returned to my friends. "It had to be done," I said. "I do not feel guilty, only drained."

"What did you do with the body?" Barsam asked.

I sat back down. "I put it in the maintenance closet and cleaned up the blood. I am hoping she is not found soon. It is the task week's end. It is time for us to plan to get Aldan and for all of us to get to the teleport machine. Tonight they will give another list of segregates; let's hope none of us are on it. It will make our mission much, much more difficult."

"What do you propose we do regarding Aldan?"

I looked at Barsam and replied, "Well, since it is the task week's end, I figured you and I would leave for the foothills tonight. We will bring him here, and then we will make our way to the machine and our future."

"Don't forget," said Barsam, "we will not be able to go near the encampment now that it is occupied. There will be guards and patrolling supervisors. We will have to get to him by an alternative route."

My stomach began to rumble violently. Suddenly I felt ravenous, and doing any constructive thinking became pretty much impossible. "I need to eat," I said. "I am going to be worthless to the cause if I don't."

Morgayne jumped up and disappeared into the food

preparation area to prepare something for me. Barsam and I continued to talk. "Get something in your stomach, and then we can take a look at the maps and find a different way to get to Aldan. But for now, you definitely need to get yourself together. Eat, calm down, and relax."

I looked at my friend's smiling face. "You have no idea how good it is to see you."

He stood and gave me a hearty pat on the shoulder. "I'm sure, brother. I'm sure."

In no time at all Morgayne was calling my name, and I went to the dining area to find fried chicken, potato root, and steaming legumes. "This looks to be the best meal the government has provided in weeks," I said. "And for the midday meal, at that! We don't eat this well while we are on tasks."

Without waiting for a response, I dug into my food. It was delightful, though I didn't know if it was delicious because it was quality or because I was starving. For the first time in what seemed like weeks I filled my belly to satisfaction, and when I was done I felt warm, full, and content. I patted my stomach and sat back in my chair.

"Thank you, Morgayne," I said.

She smiled as she cleared my dishes for cleaning. "Any time, Dyzek."

Barsam came into the dining area with the Marmaran

maps and sat down across the table from me. He spread them out on its surface so we could look at them together; then, he produced a marking pen of orange. I stood up and joined him at his side of the table.

I located the place we lived on the map. "Here we are," I began, and Dyzek silently placed a bright orange 'X' on the place. I then trailed my finger along the approximate route we had taken when we traveled to the Eloques foothills the previous week's end; Barsam marked that trail as well.

"Okay," I continued as I leaned forward and squinted my eyes at the foothills location. "I believe this is the location of Sector 3. What do you think, Barsam?"

"Yes," he agreed. "in this large basin area."

I looked closer, observing the situation of the hills around the basin area to which he was referring. "I'm sure you are correct." With that, Barsam placed an 'X' over the basin.

"So where would Aldan's place be, then?" he asked.

I continued to look, pulling memories out of the files in my mind from our journey. I then pointed at a particular hill just past the place we thought was the new encampment. "I think this is where he is holed up, right here."

Barsam studied the area a bit closer and nodded. "Even if it is not his precise location, it is very close. Close enough to determine an alternate route, Dyzek."

I looked back at the home 'X', then scanned back and forth. "How about if we take the same route, but when we get to the outermost foothills, we go due south?" I suggested, using my index finger to trace an imaginary path. "We can completely avoid the encampment while staying out of sight, just in case they are watching for anyone who approaches from a distance."

I dragged my finger south for a moment, then continued. "We will go around this foothill, and when we come to the other side we will be very, very close to Aldan, regardless of which of these hills is really his."

I lifted my finger from the final location I was signifying, and Barsam circled it not once, not twice, but three times with the orange marker. "If he wastes no time in gathering a couple of things for himself, we should be out of there quickly," I concluded. "We should add a bit more time for the trip home. Aldan will not move as fast as we do, but regardless, we should be back before the full light of day is overhead."

"If all goes as planned, we should be completely undetected," Barsam said.

"Yes," I replied. "If all goes as planned."

He took the map and folded it for the trip. We then dug the sling bags out that we had used the last time we journeyed to the foothills and made sure they had everything we needed. I put the knives I had been toting all week in my bag as well. If this day had taught me anything, it was that you never knew when you would need some kind of protection, and when it would come in seriously handy.

By the time we were satisfied with our sling bags and their contents, I wanted a nice, hot, relaxing shower. I left my friends and took one, and as I stood under the steaming stream, I thought about how far we had come since the government announced the second segregations. Even six months ago, I would not have believed our lives could, once again, become so uprooted, but here it was. I had killed another human being, and my friends and I were going to escape from the planet we called home, all just so we could be free and live our lives without fear of loss or separation.

What had happened to the people of Marmara? They were guppies, so easily convinced of the lies the Washans had told. They had become prejudiced to the point of excluding their own loved ones and imprisoning them, solely for not measuring up to invisible and phony standards. I felt tears well up once again in my eyes, and I let the water stream over my face in an attempt to stop them from falling. I was relieved and thankful that we were going to get out, or at least, that was the plan. But no matter what, I would always love and grieve the planet we were leaving.

I turned off the water and stepped out of the shower. As I stood drying my body with a towel the door opened, and in came Camira. Deep lines of concern covered her face, and when she spoke, she sounded afraid. "I told my supervisor you were ill," she began as she closed the door to the bathroom behind her. She sat on the closed lid of the toilet stool. "Since it was the task week's end, she let me leave early to come home and nurse you."

"I am not sick, Camira," I said.

She nodded, and a single tear fell from her eye. "I know. Morgayne reassured me when I got here. But she would tell me nothing else." She searched my face with her eyes. "Why would you tell me such an untruth?"

I wrapped the towel around my waist and tucked it in to hold it in place. "Because the truth would have given you massive stress. It was best to hold off until you got home."

"Well, here I am," she said. "So what is the truth?"

I opened the bathroom door. "Come with me to our

room so I can get dressed. I'm cold."

In our room, Camira sat on the bed while I took an outfit of clothing from the drawers. "I found the room with the teleporter," I began, pulling my shirt over my head. "It needed a key card for entry. I was then discovered by a Washan guard, the same one I have been seeing all week."

"Oh, no!" Camira started. "What happened?"

I shrugged a bit and avoided her eyes out of shame. "She tried to arrest me for being on that level, and I put up a fight. I ended up killing her with my knife."

Camira jumped up then and came to me quickly, wrapping her arms around me and hugging me tightly. "Dyzek! My sweet, gentle Dyzek! I am so sorry…"

I allowed her embrace and reveled in it. Once again I felt the pressure of tears behind my eyes, but I did not allow them to fall. There would be no more crying over the guard. The time for crying was over.

I returned her embrace, then pulled away. Camira searched my face yet again with her eyes, then returned to the bed and sat down. I smiled at her. "The good news is that she had a key card around her neck, and I was able to open the room to the teleporter. It is there, ready and waiting."

Now it was Camira's turn to break down in tears. Stress and relief flowed from her eyes in great drops, and I sat next to her and held her tightly. When she was finished, I said, "Barsam and I will travel to the foothills tonight to fetch Aldan. Tomorrow I will go to the museum and steal the explosive unit from the display there. We will repair it, and then I will use it to destroy the teleporter after we all transfer to the new planet."

"We will leave this weekend?" Camira asked.

I nodded and hugged her to me. "Yes. We will leave this weekend."

CHAPTER 20

Barsam and I left for the foothills right after the twenty-second hour chimed on the house timepiece. Once again we had all escaped the segregation, as none of our names were on the list during the evening announcements. I was relieved that we could carry out our plans without having to worry about that.

The girls had packed us several sandwiches once again, along with containers of water. They made sure we had enough for Aldan during the trip back as well. Both of us were in excellent spirits as we made our way through the darkness to get our new friend.

Like last time, we communicated only in whispers and low voices, and we were dressed in all black. The trip there was utterly uneventful. When we reached the detour spot, we headed south, going around the foothills we had passed through before. We could see lights reflecting off the sky in the distance this time, and we both knew they were coming from Sector 3. It was a relief to avoid them.

The detour ended up adding about a half-hour to our journey, but before we knew it, we were approaching the place where Aldan's hill was located. We weren't sure which was his in the dark, though I thought I had a pretty good idea. We ended up going around one, but it was soon apparent there was no false door anywhere on the sands of the hill.

"I think it may be this one over here," I told Barsam, and we headed to it. While it was still a bit away, I recognized a large bush as being near where we had buried Aldan's wife.

"Look here," I told him. "This is where we buried Aldan's wife. That is the hill."

We went around it, and there on the other side was the shrub-covered doorway which opened deep into the ground. Not wanting to arouse any attention from anyone that may be nearby; I took it upon myself to open the door and enter without knocking. As soon as it was ajar I could see the torches inside, and the light emanating from them was a very welcome site.

We went in and closed the door carefully behind us. I led the way down the main tunnel, and when we were far enough inside I called out, "Aldan?"

There was no response. We crept forward about twenty more feet, and I was just getting ready to call out again when a voice echoed through the chamber. "I am armed! I have a weapon! Leave now, please!"

"Aldan, it is I, Dyzek!" I was looking around furiously in the dim light, but I could not see him. "Barsam and I have come for you! We have found the teleportation device, and we want you to come with our women and us!"

Out of the shadows appeared Aldan. He held a club, resting it on his shoulder. He stepped forward cautiously. "You found it?"

I turned to him and smiled, nodding furiously. "Yes," I replied. "And the instructions, and the coordinates of the new planet."

Aldan put the club to the ground, and in the darkness I could see him smiling brightly. "I'll just grab a couple of things."

∞

The trip back bordered on being boring. We all wanted to converse, but until we were home, we knew it was not safe to behave in such a casual manner. So, we trudged along in mostly silence, stopping only once to eat and rest.

Aldan was not as slow as we thought he would be, and we made perfect time getting back. When we crept through the back and up to the window, the sun was well on the rise. Our timing couldn't have been more perfect.

We gave Aldan some clean garments to wear, and he was able to take his first real shower in years. We talked over a hot breakfast, at which time he told us about the sounds he heard consistently coming from the encampment during the day. It sounded like something out of a horror story.

"From the first light of day there are screams," he told us. "When they bring new segregates three times a week, things are quiet, but they pick up again in the morning. I think they are torturing the residents."

We all listened to Aldan and the facts he related to us, as limited as they were. When we were done eating, I stood. "I am going to get a couple of hours sleep," I said. "Tonight I am going to the museum for the explosives. Barsam, will you and the girls fill in Aldan on the plans we have established?"

Barsam nodded, then I turned to the old man. "If you have any questions for me I will meet with you when I wake. If you are tired, the girls will make up a guest bed for you to sleep in. We have a folding cot in the main closet that I believe you will find very comfortable."

It would be crucial to be well-rested before I committed the second crime of my life: the museum burglary. I knew it would be easy enough; they didn't have guards or patrols at the museum, at least not since crime had been eliminated from Marmara.

With that, I turned in, and as soon as I laid my head on my pillow, I fell into a deep sleep.

Impending Earth

CHAPTER 21

That night I suited up for the second phase of our plan. I wore my new Washan clothing, more for effect than anything. If I were discovered it wouldn't matter if I were wearing Washan attire or a potato sack, I would be in terrible trouble. Wearing the clothing would only keep me from looking suspicious at first glance.

The museum was open for visitors and tours during the daytime hours, but at night it would be completely dark. There were no alarms, so I wasn't worried about breaking in or even taking the explosive device. The most significant risk was simply avoiding being seen. The Washan uniforms I had stolen were all a dark maroon color, so I should be able to sneak around pretty much undetected.

I took the fingernail grooming kit the girls had given me for opening locks. I was sure I would need it, both for the entry and to get in the display case, but if worst came to worst I would break the glass which housed the explosives. I would then take them home where we would add a timer and a fuse. This would all be up to me, as I had extensive experience with research. I had already investigated what these old-fashioned explosives consisted of, and I knew what this unit was missing. The rest would be a matter applying what I read to the repair of the device.

The streets were empty. Being out at night for any reason other than to carry out tasks was forbidden for those in '2 of 3', so I didn't expect to see much of anybody, but I still made it a point to stay low. I traveled between buildings and hid behind trees and other large objects. It took me about three-quarters of an hour to get to the museum, ducking and dodging the way I was.

When I arrived, I didn't go up to the front entrance. Instead I went around to the rear of the building, where there was an entrance for hired task hands only. I assumed that this door would be much less secure than the main one, and when I got to it, I saw that I was correct. There was nothing more for a lock than a sliding bolt, which served more to hold the door closed than it did to lock it. I grasped the large knob on the bolt and slid it open with a bang. I tried the door, and it opened easily.

Once I was inside, I closed the door behind me and took out my small portable light. I switched it on and shone it around. I was in a back hallway; to my right was a room with a sign on the door that read, 'Authorized task hands only'. To my left was another corridor which led to the main museum and all of the displays, both historical and artistic.

It was the history section I needed to go to, and it took up the entirety of the second floor. I took the stairs off of the main display room, and within only a couple of minutes, I was standing before the glass case which held the explosives.

The unit consisted of four red sticks, which were joined together with two black strips of adhesive. Wires came out of the unit and connected to a pack of some sort; my research had told me this was a power pack, and inside were batteries. We had not used these type of power cells on Marmara for the entirety of my life, so if these were bad, I would also have to come up with an alternative means of power.

The glass casing was square, and I put one hand on either side of it. I lifted, expecting resistance, but to my surprise, it lifted easily from the display. So surprised was

I that I nearly dropped the glass. I juggled it for a moment, got a hold, and then set it carefully on the ground before I exhaled in relief.

I reached out and took hold of the explosive device gingerly. Sure, it was missing parts, but who really knew what it was still capable of doing? It wouldn't do, to go and blow myself up when I had come this far. I gently tucked it under my arm, then I went back down the stairs, through the main area, down the corridor, and out the back door.

As before, I made my way home dodging between and behind buildings and objects. I was even more careful than I was on the way to the museum because I had the device. To get caught walking off task was one thing, but to be discovered while in possession of a stolen explosive device was another entirely.

∞

"Thank the gods you are back and safe," Camira said as I climbed in through the bedroom window. It seemed to be of more use to us than the door as of late.

I hugged her and showed her the device. She looked at it as if it were an alien life form. "What is wrong with it?" she asked.

"It is missing a timer and a fuse, unless I can ensure it

has a reliable power source to set it off," I replied.

Aldan, Barsam, and Morgayne were sitting in the main area, and it appeared they were deep in conversation. When Barsam saw me, he stood immediately. "Glad you made it back! I was worried you would be seen."

"I didn't come into contact with a soul," I replied with a smile. "It went as smoothly as I could have hoped."

I closed the window coverings in the dining area for good measure, then placed the explosives down on the table. Next, I booted up the computing unit and pulled up an old diagram which explained the device and its operation. Finally, I began to compare the two, while the others either sat or stood around the table in silence.

When I was finished with that, I pulled the covering off the power pack to find it empty. There were no batteries at all inside. I thought I had an answer for this issue: a power cell from one of our personal telephone units. I would simply rig up the wiring, and the new battery should be more than sufficient.

Next, I needed a timer of some kind. "Do any of you have any ideas?"

Morgayne stood and went into the food preparation room. When she returned, she had a small screwdriver in her hand. "I think the clock timer from the meal prep machine would work, but I don't know how to get it off."

My face lit up. "Brilliant!" I took the screwdriver from her and went into the food preparation room. Within ten minutes I had the small square digital unit in my hands. I grabbed a roll of black tape from a drawer and went back to the table. Camira had already provided the battery from her personal phone device, and it too sat waiting to be added to our new weapon of destruction.

"Finally, I need something to connect the new battery," I said.

Barsam had the answer. He handed me a roll of braided cording which was nothing more than thin wire.

Once again I smiled, and then I got to work. First, I rigged up the new battery, using glue and the wire Barsam provided, which proved to be a much easier job than I expected. Next, I got the timer hooked up to the pack like a switch, and after a bit of tinkering I got it functioning. Finally, with great care, I followed the diagram, and it seemed the assembly was functional. The device would ignite itself once the timer ran out, or so we all hoped. We wouldn't be around to find out.

CHAPTER 22

Sunday Morning,

We all sat at the table in the food preparation room discussing the plan to leave Marmara.

On Sunday night we would put on the Washan uniforms, all of us but Aldan. For some reason, I had failed to consider him when I stole the garments. He would wear a black cloak and head covering, and he would steal his way to the office complex between buildings, with the others.

I would leave first, and I planned on arriving at the teleport device at the twenty-second hour precisely. I would power up the device and get the explosives ready. At the twenty-fourth hour, the others were to arrive, and I would send them, one at a time, to our new home, that strange new planet in an entirely peculiar galaxy.

Barsam would go first, just in case, there was danger

there. He would take nothing more with him than a makeshift mace, which was merely a club with a knife attached. He would be followed by Aldan, who would assist him in preparing for the arrival of the women. I would be last. I would set the explosive device and then teleport myself to our new planet, the new Marmara.

But we would not call it Marmara. We determined it would be called 'Earth', meaning 'planet' in old speak.

I left at half past the twenty-first hour, on foot, nothing with me but my sling bag, which held everything I would need to get things up and running down on the second lower level of the Elite/Washan offices. I had my knives, the explosives, the operating instructions, and the coordinates of our new home.

At first, I walked the streets, but at a distance, I saw patrolling supervisors walking the streets near the outskirts of '2 of 3', so I ducked between a couple of residences and began to walk around the back perimeter. Once I got to the Elite sector, '1 of 3', the patrollers would be gone. The Elite did not have to live under such supervision.

The offices came into sight around three-quarters past the hour, and soon I was there. The main doors were locked, as we all knew they would be. We had already planned for this. We would be entering through the rear entrance, which was once again used by Elite task hands only. Just as I thought, the rear door was completely unsecured.

I entered the building and wound my way through the back corridors. After turning only two corners, I found myself in the main entryway, only about twenty feet from the lift. I boarded and pressed the button, directing the elevator to take me down.

The door opened, and I got off and walked directly to the teleportation room. I rummaged through my sling bag until my hand closed around the key card. I swiped it once, and red light turned to green. The door popped open and swung ajar, inviting me in.

The teleporter stood at the end of the room, lit up inside and lights flashing. I walked up to the podium with the panel, and then I fished the operational instructions out of my bag. As I laid them out, I glanced at my timepiece: five minutes past the hour.

The instructions said that the machine had to 'power up'. I began to flip the switches and press the buttons that were appropriate, and soon a loud hum filled the air. The inner light, which had already been lit, grew even brighter, and an arch with lights over the door of the machine came on in synchronized harmony.

It was now on, and it appeared to be doing everything it was supposed to.

I would not enter the coordinates quite yet. I had a bit of time, so I left the room, propping the door open with my sling bag. I walked down to the maintenance closet and stared at the door for a moment, building my courage. Finally, I took a deep breath and grasped the knob and opened the door.

The smell of rotting flesh hit me in the face, and my hand flew up to cover my mouth and nose. So strong was it that my eyes were watering, and I had to fight not to gag from the stench. I reached around the corner and pressed the button to turn on the lights. There lay the dead guard, blood pooled all around her. It had begun to run down the drain in the floor but had congealed before it could.

I turned the light off and backed out of the closet, my stomach sick with my own murderous sin. I knew with surety that it had had to be done if I wanted to live if I wanted my loved ones to live, but that fact didn't make what I had done any easier to bear. I felt terribly guilty.

I shut the door and looked at my timepiece again. It was twenty-five minutes past the hour now. I would set about entering the galaxial coordinates and preparing the bomb.

I walked into the teleporter room again and began tapping in the proper codes as Camira had written them down for me. The process of entering the coordinates took much longer than I anticipated; there was much more to it than merely punching buttons. Specific switches needed to be flipped at specific times, and twice I had to start the process over.

Finally, I was finished, and I looked at my timepiece yet again. It was now ten minutes until the hour. My companions would all be arriving soon.

Now I took the explosives and rigged them up, attaching them with more of the wire I had used for the battery to the outside of the teleporter itself. I would not set the timer until the others were already gone. The explosives were old and could be touchy. I would not risk blowing up anyone but myself by accident. I would set it, and once I knew it was counting down, I would teleport myself and join the others.

Just as I finished securing the explosives, I heard the lift kick in. It was coming down. My friends had arrived.

I went into the corridor and watched the indicator as the lift descended. The doors opened, and Camira and Morgayne came rushing out, stricken looks on their faces.

"Where is…" I turned and looked inside the lift.

Barsam was struggling to get off. Because he was fighting to hold up Aldan, who appeared to be barely able to walk.

"We were spotted, Dyzek," Barsam began. "We all started to run, but the patroller took chase. They used a weapon of electricity on Aldan, and I could not get him to wake up."

He lowered the limp body of Aldan to the floor. I knelt next to him and put my head against his chest. His heart was beating, but it was erratic and faint.

"Were you followed?" I asked.

Morgayne was weeping, but Camira had her wits about her. "No," she said. Barsam stabbed the patroller with his knife…many, many times."

"I had to leave the body there," Barsam said. "It will surely be found. They will know there has been a defiant uprising of some kind. We must move now!"

I stood and went to the lift panel. All I could think to do was dismantle the power to the lift. It wouldn't stop anyone, but it would undoubtedly slow down people with intent to prevent our escape.

I pulled the panel off of the wall using my knife and proceeded to cut through the wires. Sparks flew, and I got a couple of small burns, but the lights shut down, and the power left the lift audibly.

I turned to my friends. "It's time for us to get moving

now. Grab Aldan; I will send him through second, just as we have planned."

They followed me down the corridor and into the teleportation room. The red light on the podium panel had turned a bright green, and I knew the device was powered up and ready to go. I knew that we were supposed to wait three minutes between sends, but we had already agreed we would not wait more than needed to allow for re-powering.

"Okay, Barsam," I said to my friend, "Are you ready?"

He nodded, his eyes wide. "As ready as I will ever be, brother."

He stepped through the door of the unit, weapon in his hands. He then leaned out and gave Morgayne a long kiss. "I will see you soon, love."

"Soon," she repeated, and with tears in her eyes she stepped back and went to Camira for strength and comfort.

Barsam closed the door, pulling on it until it latched. I winked at him and nodded, and he returned the gestures before closing his eyes in fear and anticipation. I gave the girls and a limp Aldan only a glance before I pressed the large red button with the flat of my palm. It compressed easily, and light as bright as lightning, and just about as powerful filled the teleporter compartment.

It was blinding, and to be honest, it took my breath away. All of us, with the exception of Aldan, covered our eyes against it. Then, just as quickly as it appeared, it was gone, and the teleport unit was empty.

"It worked," I said, almost to myself. "Barsam is gone."

We all just stood and stared at the empty place where my friend had stood. Finally, after a few minutes, I snapped myself out of it. "I need to power it up again," I mumbled, and began flipping switches and pressing buttons.

The girls gave their attention to Aldan, who seemed to come alive after we sent Barsam. Maybe all the power in the air jolted him back to life, but who knew? I was just glad he was alert again.

The next few minutes passed in an instant, and Aldan took his turn. I repowered, waited, and then we sent Morgayne. After repowering yet again, Camira and I focused our attention on each other.

"I love you, Dyzek," she said to me with a smile.

"And I you, Camira," I replied. "Don't fret now. I will be right behind you."

We held each other for what seemed like seconds but was actually quite some time. Then we heard a loud crash that appeared to be coming from the level above. It was followed by voices that were angry and desperate. Frantically I pressed the button to let the teleporter recharge.

More loud crashes followed, and I knew they were coming down by way of the emergency staircase at the end of the corridor. I looked at Camira, my eyes flashing. "Go!"

Sending Camira to safety, I quickly hit the transport button and proceeded to begin the recharge sequence. I ran down to the end of the corridor and using the wire I kept in my trouser pocket, hastily I popped the lock on the room with the canned goods.

Furiously I began to drag the boxes. Then I stacked them before the staircase doorway. I had it nearly covered, and I was bringing out one final box when the men tried to open the door. The boxes shifted, but they were too heavy to move with the door.

"They are down here," one of the men screamed. "They have barricaded the door!"

They continued to push with all their might against it, and I knew I was out of time. I ran down the hall to the teleporter room, then secured the door tightly behind me with a large metal chair, wedged under the doorknob.

The green light shone brightly. It was powered up.

I set the timer on the bomb. Rather than thirty minutes, I set it for two. I disguised the bomb as a trashcan, just in case they managed to get in, then I ran inside and shut the door tightly. I took the small remote in my hand. Then, I looked down and smiled.

"Here we go," I said.

With that, I closed my eyes tightly and pressed my thumb down on the button on the remote, and the lightning flashed, sending me to oblivion.

CHAPTER 23

I sit on the step of the home I built with my bare hands. It is a beautiful sunny day, with a sky as blue as my eyes, and a warm breeze that ruffles my hair. Camira is in a patch of flowers, picking them and lying them in a bundle. She will put them in water and place them here and there around the house to brighten it up. She does this every day.

In the distance, I see my friend and brother, Barsam. He is working the ground and tending crops. He loves to do this, and it brings him vast amounts of satisfaction.

Morgayne feeds the animals that we keep for food. Chickens, cows, and pigs. We keep only enough to feed us, for that is all we need. I watch her as she scatters seed on the ground before the chickens, and I can hear her singing. Her belly is great with a child, and we are all excited to meet the newest resident of Earth.

Aldan has been ill recently and has taken to his bed. We all care for him, and he has taught us much about working the land and animals. Having him has been a blessing, though I do not expect him to be with us much longer. We all try to keep him as content and comfortable as possible.

We all know peace, love, and happiness. No one ever followed us through the teleport. At least, if they did, we have not encountered them yet.

I often wonder what happened to our old home, and to the Washans. I wonder if the quasar hit yet. I wonder if the teleporter was destroyed by the explosives. I wonder if the dirty Washans have taken over completely.

Then I remind myself that it doesn't matter. Earth is our home now, and we are happy. If anyone tries to infiltrate what we have created, I will take out a blind rage on them, and they will cease to exist. When I think of this, I rest easy.

But sometimes, I dream of Marmara. In my dream, I am a hostage, and I am watching a massive quasar shoot through the sky. It is coming for me.

I am always blessed to wake up at home.

REQUISITION

If you enjoyed this novel, please consider writing a review on what you thought, and giving a rating, or any suggestion. Please tell your friends and loved ones.

Thank You Greatly

- J.R. Clark

ABOUT THE AUTHOR

My name is Jonathan, this is my first novel. I am an aspiring photographer, videographer, graphic designer, website designer, and now author. As of writing this book, I am 14 years old, and two grades ahead in school. Someday I hope to make a movie, whether it be any of my own work such as this one or, for another piece of literature. I believe in quality before quantity.